YORK NOTES

A VIEW FROM THE BRIDGE

ARTHUR MILLER

NOTES BY SHAY DALY

Longman
is an imprint of

PEARSON

York Press

YORK PRESS
322 Old Brompton Road, London SW5 9JH

PEARSON EDUCATION LIMITED
Edinburgh Gate, Harlow,
Essex CM20 2JE, United Kingdom
Associated companies, branches and representatives throughout the world

First published 1997
New edition 2002
This new and fully revised edition 2011

10 9 8 7 6 5 4 3

ISBN 978–1–4082–7001–1

Illustrated by Jo Blake; and Neil Gower (p. 6)

Photograph of Arthur Miller reproduced by kind permission of Alamy Limited

Phototypeset by Pantek Arts Ltd, Maidstone
Printed in China (CTPS/03)

Contents

PART ONE: INTRODUCTION

Study and revision advice

There are two main stages to your reading and work on *A View from the Bridge*. Firstly, the study of the play as you read it. Secondly, your preparation or revision for the exam. These top tips will help you with both.

 **READING AND STUDYING THE PLAY – DEVELOP INDEPENDENCE!**

- Try to engage and respond **personally** to the characters, ideas and action – not just for your enjoyment, but also because it helps you develop your own **independent ideas** and **thoughts** about *A View from the Bridge*. This is something that examiners are very keen to see.

- **Talk** about the text with friends and family; ask questions in class; put forward your own viewpoint – and, if you have time, **read around** the text to find out about *A View from the Bridge*.

- Take time to **consider** and **reflect** about the **key elements** of the play; keep your own notes, mind-maps, diagrams, scribbled jottings about the characters and how you respond to them; follow the story as it progresses (what do you think might happen?); discuss the main themes and ideas (what do *you* think it is about? Pride? Justice? The law?); pick out language that impresses you or makes an **impact**, and so on.

- Treat your studying **creatively**. When you write essays or give talks about the play make your responses creative. Think about using really clear ways of explaining yourself, use unusual quotations, well-chosen vocabulary, and try powerful, persuasive ways of beginning or ending what you say or write.

 **REVISION – DEVELOP ROUTINES AND PLANS!**

- **Good revision** comes from **good planning**. Find out when your exam is and then plan to look at key aspects of *A View from the Bridge* on different days or times during your revision period. You could use these Notes – see **How can these Notes help me?** – and add dates or times when you are going to cover a particular topic.

- Use **different ways** of **revising**. Sometimes talking about the text and what you know/don't know with a friend or member of the family can help; at other times, filling a sheet of A4 with all your ideas in different coloured pens about a character, for example Eddie, can make ideas come alive; other times, making short lists of quotations to learn, or numbering events in the plot can assist you.

- **Practise plans** and **essays**. As you get nearer the 'day', start by looking at essay **questions** and writing short bulleted plans. Do several plans (you don't have to write the whole essay); then take those plans and add details to them (quotations, linked ideas). Finally, using the advice in **Part Six: Grade Booster**, write some practice essays and then check them out against the advice we have provided.

 **EXAMINER'S TIP**

Prepare for the exam/ assessment! Whatever you need to bring, make sure you have it with you – books, if you're allowed, pens, pencils – and that you turn up on time!

Introducing *A View from the Bridge*

SETTING

A View from the Bridge is set in Red Hook, Brooklyn, New York in the late 1940s. The action mostly takes place in the Carbones' living room and dining room in a tenement block.

CHARACTERS: WHO'S WHO

ALFIERI

EDDIE

BEATRICE

CATHERINE

MARCO

RODOLPHO

LOUIS

MIKE

ARTHUR MILLER: AUTHOR AND CONTEXT

1915 Arthur Miller born 17 October in New York

1918 End of the First World War

1939–45 Second World War

1945 Atomic bombs dropped on Hiroshima and Nagasaki by the Americans

1947 Arthur Miller completes *All My Sons*, his first major success, and wins a Tony award for the play

1949 *Death of a Salesman* wins the Pulitzer prize

1950 Arthur Miller summoned by Senator McCarthy to name Communist sympathisers. He refuses. The fine he receives is later quashed by the Supreme Court

1953 Writes *The Crucible*

1956 Marries the film star Marilyn Monroe

2005 Arthur Miller dies on 11 February

PART TWO: PLOT AND ACTION

Plot summary: What happens in *A View from the Bridge*?

REVISION ACTIVITY

- Go through the summary boxes below and **highlight** what you think is the **key moment** in each section.

- Then find each moment in the **text** and **reread** it. Write down **two reasons** why you think each moment is so **important**.

ACT ONE

Part One (pp. 3–22)

- Alfieri, the lawyer, enters and sets the scene. He tells the audience that justice is very important to the people of Red Hook and that often justice is quite different to the law.

- Enter Eddie Carbone. He annoys his niece Catherine when he criticises her clothes and her behaviour.

- Beatrice, Eddie's wife, is worried because of the imminent arrival of her cousins who are illegal immigrants from Sicily.

- Eddie encourages Beatrice to tell Catherine the story of Vinny Bolzano who informed on his uncle who was an illegal immigrant.

- The cousins, Marco and Rodolfo, arrive.

- Eddie shows his dislike of Rodolfo.

Part Two (pp. 22–35)

- Alfieri talks to the audience about Eddie's troubled future.

- Eddie shows how irritated he is by Rodolfo.

- Beatrice argues that Eddie is being unreasonable and tells him that he should not create any trouble.

- She speaks to him about the problems they have in their relationship and also about the fact that she no longer feels like 'a wife' (p. 24).

- Rodolfo returns from a night out with Catherine. Eddie tells Catherine that Rodolfo is using her to help him become an American citizen.

- When Beatrice is alone with Catherine she points out that Catherine is now a grown woman and she should behave appropriately in Eddie's company.

- Eddie meets Alfieri and tries to enlist his help but the lawyer tells Eddie there is nothing he can do.

Part Three (pp. 35–42)

- Marco and Rodolfo relate some of their experiences in Italy.
- Eddie interjects with some negative comments that disturb the pleasant mood. He tells Rodolfo that he is breaking the American code of morality.
- Catherine flirts with Rodolfo to show her independence.
- While showing Rodolfo how to box, Eddie hits him.
- Marco reacts by lifting a chair with one hand to show his superior strength over Eddie.

ACT TWO

Part One (pp. 43–58)

- Catherine and Rodolfo are alone in the apartment. They talk about their future.
- Rodolfo attempts to persuade Catherine to break free from Eddie's influence.
- Eddie returns and sees Catherine first, and then Rodolfo emerging from the bedroom.
- In a drunken rage he orders Rodolfo to leave. He then kisses Catherine on the mouth.
- When Rodolfo flies to her defence, Eddie kisses him also.
- Eddie revisits Alfieri who warns him not to inform the Immigration Bureau about Rodolfo and Marco.
- Eddie ignores his advice and calls the Bureau.
- The immigration officers arrive and arrest Marco and Rodolfo.
- Marco suspects Eddie and spits in his face.
- Eddie threatens to kill Marco.

Part Two (pp. 58–64)

- In the prison reception room Alfieri says he will bail Marco if he promises not to kill Eddie. Eventually Marco promises.
- At home Eddie says he will not be satisfied till Marco apologises to him.
- Beatrice confronts Eddie about his feelings for Catherine.
- Marco appears and Eddie demands he give him back his good name.
- They clash and Eddie dies from a wound inflicted by his own knife.
- Alfieri mourns Eddie and says that it is better to 'settle for half' (p. 64) rather than always demanding full justice.

Act One, Part 1: The Carbones await the arrival of the Italians (pp. 3–8)

SUMMARY

① Alfieri, the lawyer, enters. He talks about the distrust felt for all lawyers in Red Hook where the play is set.

② Alfieri speaks about justice and the law which are important themes in the play.

③ Eddie Carbone, 'a longshoreman' (p. 4) goes into his house where he talks to Beatrice, his wife and Catherine, his niece.

④ Catherine is upset when Eddie criticises her clothes and her behaviour.

⑤ Eddie informs Beatrice and Catherine that Marco and Rodolfo, Beatrice's cousins, have arrived on board ship from Sicily. They are illegal immigrants.

⑥ Beatrice is very nervous. She is worried in case the cousins do not find the place acceptable.

⑦ Eddie warns Beatrice and Catherine that they should be cautious and not say anything about Marco and Rodolfo.

⑧ Catherine then prepares Eddie for some big news of her own.

WHY IS THIS SECTION IMPORTANT?

A It establishes **the setting** – a tenement in Red Hook, near Brooklyn Bridge in New York.

B We are introduced to some of the **main characters** – Alfieri, Eddie, Catherine and Beatrice.

C You see Eddie's **over-protectiveness** of his niece, Catherine.

D The playwright lets the audience know that the **illegal immigrants** will arrive very soon and this creates **excitement and tension** for Beatrice and Catherine.

THE SETTING

The play is set in Red Hook in Brooklyn. Red Hook, where the Carbones live, is a slum area. It is worth reading the introductory stage directions to get a feel for the simple way the characters live.

The very first scene is located outside Eddie's tenement and this helps to give a feeling for the wider community. This is also the setting where the final action of the play takes place.

The rest of the action in this section takes place in the Carbones' living room and dining room and is, as Arthur Miller says, *'clean, sparse and homely'* (p. 3). This complements the lives of the family who are very simple people.

CHARACTERS – ALFIERI, EDDIE CARBONE, BEATRICE AND CATHERINE

In this opening section the playwright introduces Alfieri as both a character in the play and also as a narrator who speaks directly to the audience. He is a thoughtful man who is obviously sympathetic towards the community he serves.

Eddie is an ordinary man who works on the ships. He shows us his protective attitude towards Catherine when he says, 'You're gettin' to be a big girl now, you gotta keep yourself more, you can't be so friendly, kid' (p. 6). Here he is seen as a strong family man.

Catherine is a lively, attractive and very warm character. Even though she is slightly annoyed with Eddie when he criticises her, she tries to lighten the mood by saying, 'Eddie, I wish there was one guy you couldn't tell me things about!' (p. 6).

Beatrice has a generous nature and that is the reason she has invited Marco and Rodolfo to stay in their flat. She shows a certain nervousness, however, when she hears they have arrived.

EXAMINER'S TIP: WRITING ABOUT THE ILLEGAL IMMIGRANTS

It is important to realise that the Red Hook community believes that there is nothing wrong with the practice of sheltering illegal immigrants and that it is the duty of all neighbours to help protect them.

You will notice that Eddie is completely relaxed about the situation when he tells Catherine and Beatrice that the cousins have arrived. This tells the audience that it is a regular occurrence that Eddie sees every day.

Beatrice appears to be more worried about the lack of food and the state of the flat than she is about breaking the law. Catherine is merely excited that two relatives are coming to stay.

GLOSSARY

longshoreman a person who works on the docks

Act One, Part 2: Eddie objects to Catherine leaving (pp. 9–15)

KEY QUOTE

Eddie: 'I don't care who sees them goin' in and out so long as you don't see them goin' in and out.'

KEY QUOTE

Beatrice: 'Who's mad? I'm not mad. You're the one is mad.'

GRADE BOOSTER

Look at the way the playwright creates the relationship between Eddie and Catherine in the first section. What do you notice about it?

SUMMARY

1. Eddie immediately raises objections when he hears that Catherine wants to go to work in the office of a plumbing company near the Navy Yard.

2. Eddie says he wants Catherine to complete her education and that he doesn't like the sailors and plumbers that she will meet.

3. Beatrice becomes angry when Eddie rejects her advice to let Catherine have her freedom.

4. Beatrice eventually persuades Eddie to let Catherine go out to work and the girl reacts very emotionally.

5. For a moment there is real warmth and good humour while Eddie allows them to be a family. However, he does say how much he will miss Catherine.

6. The imminent arrival of the cousins changes the atmosphere as Catherine worries about hiding their identity.

7. With Eddie's prompting, Beatrice tells the story of the informer, Vinny Bolzano, and how he became an outcast, for informing on his uncle.

8. There is a quiet moment when Eddie turns to Catherine and says he never expected her to grow up.

9. When she leaves the room Eddie asks Beatrice why she is always angry with him these days. Beatrice denies this.

WHY IS THIS SECTION IMPORTANT?

A The audience is aware of **Eddie's reluctance** to let Catherine go.

B Beatrice's **strength of character** is shown when she stands up to Eddie and he accepts that she is right.

C Catherine's **unselfishness** is obvious when she is more **concerned** for the **immigrants** than she is for herself.

D The story of **Vinny Bolzano** creates a basis for the irony which will be created when Eddie turns informer himself later in the play.

E **Tension** between Eddie and Beatrice is revealed.

EDDIE AND CATHERINE – A CONTRAST

Eddie's vulnerability is clearly shown. We see that he appears lost when he hears that Catherine is going out to work. He repeats the same arguments over and over: 'Please, do me a favour, will ya? I want you to be with different kind of people' (p. 10) and in the end he says, 'And then you'll move away' (p. 11). He is totally caught up in her leaving and can't stand the thought of it. There is something pathetic in his comment, 'I guess I just never figured on one thing ... That you would ever grow up' (p. 15).

Catherine is not fully aware of Eddie's sense of loss but she does feel for him and tries to reassure him when she says, 'You sound like I'm goin' a million miles!' (p. 15). The moment of intimacy, when she lights his cigar for him, shows her innocence and naivety. She loves her uncle and, unlike Beatrice, she can't see how obsessive he is about her.

THE STORY OF VINNY BOLZANO

This simple story will resonate throughout Act Two, when Eddie makes the phone call setting the foundations for what is to follow. Catherine reacts with utter revulsion when Beatrice tells her what happened to the Bolzanos. Here, disbelievingly, she says, 'The kid snitched?' (p. 13) and a little later, 'What, was he crazy?' (p. 14). All three of them are horrified by what Vinny did, and the story is a warning that they must all be very careful not to reveal the whereabouts of Marco and Rodolfo. It also shows the closeness of the community that will discard anybody who breaks the code. The fact that they are breaking the law by harbouring illegal immigrants does not affect them as codes of honour and community spirit are more important. This refers back to what Alfieri said at the beginning of Act 1: 'A lawyer means the law, and in Sicily, from where their fathers came, the law has not been a friendly idea since the Greeks were beaten' (p. 4).

EXAMINER'S TIP: WRITING ABOUT BEATRICE'S FUNCTION IN THIS SECTION

Beatrice is, in some ways, the female version of Alfieri because, like him, she can see what is happening to Eddie. However, instead of talking about what should happen, she does something about it.

Unlike Eddie, Beatrice is utterly selfless. She tries to protect Eddie from himself. She protects Catherine from Eddie's obsessiveness and she prepares her apartment for the two illegal immigrants. We are aware that she oversees everything and does her best to ensure that there is balance and harmony. She appreciates what Eddie is doing for her cousins and she lets him know this when she says, 'Mmm! You're an angel! God'll bless you. You'll see, you'll get a blessing for this!' (p. 8).

Beatrice is the voice of reason against Eddie's unreasonableness and Catherine's wide-eyed innocence. She knows that she must calm what could be a very volatile situation.

GRADE BOOSTER

The relationship between Beatrice and Eddie is complex here. There are times when they are quite comfortable with one another, but there are times also when there is tension between them. Look out for evidence of tension in this section and throughout the play.

CHECKPOINT 2

How do you explain Eddie's contradictory feelings for Catherine?

GRADE BOOSTER

Examine the way Miller creates the aggression that is part of Eddie's character. How does this aggression prepare the audience for what happens later?

Act One, Part 3: The Italians arrive (pp. 15–22)

SUMMARY

1. Alfieri tells the audience that Beatrice's 'cousins' (p.15) docked at ten o'clock.

2. Marco and Rodolfo, the Italian immigrants, arrive escorted by Tony, a longshoreman, who makes it quite clear they are now on their own and must go to work.

3. They receive a warm welcome from Beatrice, Eddie and Catherine. Marco assures Eddie that they will not outstay their welcome.

4. The men describe the work in Italy, Marco seriously but Rodolfo laughing all the time.

5. Marco is delighted when he learns how much they will earn because he has a wife and family to support back in Italy.

6. When Catherine asks Rodolfo if he is married, he says he is too poor to marry. He wants to buy a powerful motorbike and return to Italy.

7. Rodolfo's vibrant good humour and comic turn of phrase is appreciated by Beatrice and Catherine but not by Eddie.

8. Rodolfo's singing of 'Paper Doll' makes Eddie feel very uncomfortable. He rudely interrupts by threatening him that people will be suspicious.

9. Eddie continues his belligerent behaviour by insisting that Catherine change her shoes.

CHECKPOINT 3

Why does Eddie feel uncomfortable when Rodolfo begins to sing?

KEY QUOTE

Catherine: (*enthralled*) 'Leave him finish, it's beautiful!' (*To Beatrice*) 'He's terrific! It's terrific, Rodolfo.'

CHECKPOINT 4

Why does Eddie ask Catherine to remove her high heels?

WHY IS THIS SECTION IMPORTANT?

A Arthur Miller very quickly **establishes** the **characters** of **Marco** and **Rodolfo** and lets us see how very **different** they are. They are also both strongly connected to the theme of **law** and **justice**.

B **Catherine's attraction** for **Rodolfo** is shown through her total fascination with him and everything about him.

C We see the beginning of **Eddie's hostility** towards Rodolfo when he tells him to stop singing.

D Miller allows us to see **Marco's quiet authority** when he speaks to Rodolfo after Eddie appeals to him.

E There is already **evidence** of how **petty Eddie can be** when he tells Catherine to remove her high heels.

LAW AND JUSTICE IN *A VIEW FROM THE BRIDGE*

Law and justice are important themes that run through the play. The law is being broken when Marco and Rodolfo arrive but, at the same time, justice, as understood by the people of Red Hook, demands that they are protected from the authorities. Alfieri touches on these themes in his opening speech. The law is looked on with suspicion but justice is very important. Justice, Alfieri says, was often achieved by breaking the law but he feels that seeking total justice is an uncomfortable way to live. He, himself, is happy to 'settle for half' (p. 4).

GRADE BOOSTER

It's important to remember that the playwright has carefully constructed both the characters and the language they speak. Try analysing the way in which Miller creates a change of atmosphere with just a few lines of dialogue.

Alfieri senses that there is a timeless quality about this story. Perhaps, he thinks, this same sort of struggle for justice was dealt with by another lawyer two thousand years ago, implying that this type of conflict happens in every era and in every community throughout the world.

THE RELATIONSHIP BETWEEN CATHERINE AND RODOLFO BEGINS

From the moment the two men enter, Catherine shows no interest in Marco, only Rodolfo. She comments on how blond Rodolfo is. When she asks Rodolfo if he is married, her question may be just a request for information but the audience will feel that there is something deeper going on here. Her interest increases when she discovers he can sing, and Rodolfo shows his first real connection with Catherine when he accedes to her request to sing 'Paper Doll' (p. 21). His interest becomes a little more obvious when he looks at Catherine when she enters from the bedroom. 'Yes,' ([he] *laughs, indicating Catherine*) 'especially when they [girls] are so beautiful' (p. 22).

KEY QUOTE

Eddie: 'What's the high heels for, Garbo?'

DID YOU KNOW

The main characters in all Arthur Miller's major plays are ordinary men who live ordinary lives. Willy Loman in *Death of a Salesman*, John Proctor in *The Crucible*, Joe Keller in *All My Sons*, and, of course, Eddie in *A View from the Bridge* – they all, as Miller says about Eddie, allow themselves 'to be wholly known' and they all die at the end.

EXAMINER'S TIP: WRITING ABOUT EDDIE'S GROWING HOSTILITY

You should be aware of how expertly Miller builds the aggressive nature of Eddie's behaviour and also how quickly he establishes how volatile he can be. In the middle of Rodolfo's song the playwright shows us how unsettled Eddie is when the stage directions indicate that: *'Eddie rises and moves upstage'* (p. 21). When he interrupts Rodolfo he is very sharp. At no point does he use his name, instead calling him 'kid' (p. 21). Superficially it seems he is preventing him from singing for his own safety but already we are aware that there is something more bubbling under the surface, especially when Miller tells us that Eddie's *'face (is) puffed with trouble'* (p. 22). If asked about Eddie's hostility towards Rodolfo you should be aware of the way Miller creates this animosity quite early on in the play so that we are prepared for what happens later.

Act One, Part 4: Eddie's hostility towards Rodolfo grows (pp. 22–35)

SUMMARY

1. Alfieri suggests to the audience that Eddie's life will never be the same again.

2. Eddie is upset that Rodolfo is spending so much of his time on public show, so much time singing and, above all, spending so much time with Catherine.

3. Louis and Mike, longshoremen, talk to Eddie about Marco, whom they admire, and Rodolfo, whom makes them laugh. Eddie is uncomfortable during this conversation.

4. Beatrice tells Eddie that he is jealous of Rodolfo and that his interest in the issue of Catherine and Rodolfo is unhealthy.

5. Beatrice tries to discuss the flaws in their own relationship but Eddie walks out.

6. Eddie tells Catherine that Rodolfo is only interested in her because he wants to be an American citizen. This upsets Catherine.

7. Beatrice tells Catherine that she must break free from Eddie in order to be more independent, more grown up.

8. Eddie visits Alfieri and tries to persuade him that Rodolfo is breaking the law. The lawyer tells Eddie that the only point of law that can be addressed is that of illegal immigration.

9. Eddie now seems to be on the brink of desperation and Alfieri is aware that Eddie is about to destroy himself and those close to him.

> ★ **GRADE BOOSTER**
>
> Many examiners say that it is best to say a lot about a little. In other words you should choose small sections of dialogue and analyse them in depth rather than attempt to write about the whole play.

> **CHECKPOINT 5**
>
> What does Eddie mean when he says: 'He ain't supposed to go advertising himself'? (p. 22).

WHY IS THIS SECTION IMPORTANT?

A **Eddie's hostility** towards Rodolfo has hardened and he does not seem capable of thinking about anything else.

B We see **Beatrice confronting Eddie** about their own **relationship** and about his unhealthy interest in Catherine. This raises the level of **tension**.

C **Catherine** is **deeply affected** by Eddie's accusations, showing the power Eddie has.

D Eddie's **desperation** is obvious when he visits **Alfieri** and implies there should be a legal way of **getting rid of Rodolfo**.

E As an **audience** we begin to see the **significance** of the **Vinny Bolzano story** and Miller creates a sense of **foreboding**.

EDDIE'S HOSTILITY INCREASES

The undercurrent of the exchange between Eddie and his workmates sets him on edge. This conversation, the previous accusation by Beatrice and now the excited laughter of Catherine as she returns with Rodolfo, are all frustrations that Eddie allows to fuel his inner hostility. He slanders Rodolfo to Catherine when he questions the young man's motives for wanting a relationship with her. Catherine breaks down in the face of his onslaught and she attempts to shut him out. Eddie seems about to explode.

E<small>DDIE'S</small> <small>FRUSTRATION</small>

The audience now hears Eddie say what is, perhaps, his most significant pronouncement so far: 'But I know what they're laughin' at, and when I think of that guy layin' his hands on her I could – I mean it's eatin' me out, Mr Alfieri, because I struggled for that girl. And now he comes in my house and – ' (p. 33).

Eddie's frustration is embodied in these lines. He feels a desperation which he cannot fully verbalise, but it is possible that the audience can sense what he is really saying – that Catherine is rejecting Eddie, a real man who 'struggled' for her, unlike this effeminate boy. He believes that a huge injustice has been inflicted on him.

E<small>XAMINER'S TIP</small>: W<small>RITING ABOUT</small> E<small>DDIE AND</small> A<small>LFIERI</small>

If you can analyse what Eddie is saying to Alfieri in this section you will be able to write about how unreasonable Eddie has become. It will be helpful if you can compare what he is saying with Alfieri's reasoned arguments. Eddie is asking Alfieri if there is a law that can stop Rodolfo marrying Catherine. He is not prepared to listen when Alfieri tells him that there is no such law.

CHECKPOINT 6

What is Eddie's real reason for suggesting that Rodolfo is a 'weird'?

CHECKPOINT 7

Why is Catherine upset by the suggestion that Rodolfo wants to become an American citizen?

KEY QUOTE

Eddie: 'You mean it's all right with you? That's gonna be her husband?'

Act One, Part 5: Marco confronts Eddie (pp. 35–42)

SUMMARY

1. Eddie continues to control the atmosphere when he kills the relaxed mood of the family.

2. Marco says he is happy that he can send money to his wife but he misses her and his children. Eddie compounds Marco's misery when he suggests Marco's wife might be unfaithful.

3. Rodolfo tells Eddie that they have a strict code of conduct in his country. Eddie seizes the opportunity to tell Rodolfo that he is breaking the American code when he takes Catherine out without his permission.

4. Marco supports Eddie.

5. Beatrice encourages Catherine's show of independence when the girl asks Rodolfo to dance.

6. Eddie attempts to assert himself over Rodolfo by suggesting that Rodolfo's skills show that he is not manly. When he tears the newspaper in two he is implying that he could easily do the same to the Italian.

7. Eddie strikes Rodolfo when attempting to teach him how to box. Marco lifts a chair above Eddie's head to show that he is stronger than Eddie.

CHECKPOINT 8

What, according to Eddie, is the American code and why does he say that Rodolfo is breaking it?

WHY IS THIS SECTION IMPORTANT?

A Alfieri begins to **prepare the audience** for the tragedy to come.

B Eddie's cunning is displayed when he **attempts** to **manipulate Marco and Rodolfo**.

C To begin with, Eddie is unaware that he is dealing with a **much stronger character** in **Marco**.

D **Beatrice** continues to encourage and **support Catherine** in her show of independence.

E **Marco's display of strength** has **echoes** of what is to come at the **end** of the play.

CHECKPOINT 9

Identify Alfieri's function in the play.

TRIAL OF STRENGTH

The trial of strength is full of tension and pathos. While Eddie 'teaches' Rodolfo to box, the tension is shown through the reactions of the other characters in the scene:

- Beatrice, after her initial alarm, sees only what she considers friendly rivalry.

- Catherine is fearful for Rodolfo's safety. Much as she is fond of Eddie, she is showing that, if necessary, she will take Rodolfo's part.

- Marco is cautious at first but then decides to react. He sees Eddie's action as hostile and, without saying so, he challenges Eddie to a trial of strength.

KEY QUOTE

Eddie: 'It's wonderful. He sings, he cooks, he could make dresses …'

GRADE BOOSTER

Eddie lists all of Rodolfo's skills. You should be able to say what this tells us about Eddie and what these skills tell us about Rodolfo.

Simple though it seems, this scene is important because it shows that, when it really matters, Marco will always be the stronger of the two men. He will be loyal to Rodolfo and if Eddie shows further aggression towards either of the brothers Marco will be a force to be reckoned with.

EXAMINER'S TIP: WRITING ABOUT BEATRICE AS THE CALMING VOICE

Beatrice is usually aware of Eddie's attempts to create a hostile mood and tries to head him off before he can create chaos. When Eddie shows his annoyance, after Catherine and Rodolfo come back late, she tries to plead their case. Except for one brief moment when she tells Eddie: 'Well then, be an uncle then.' (*Eddie looks at her, aware of her criticising force*)' (p. 38), she is reason itself.

Remember: do not write about the characters as if they are real people. Be aware that they are the creations of the playwright and you will gain more marks if you analyse the way he shapes them.

EXAMINER'S TIP

Read all parts of the question carefully to ensure you answer them fully. Underline key words in the question.

Act Two, Part 1: Eddie tells Rodolfo to leave (pp. 43–8)

SUMMARY

① Alfieri ends his introduction to Act Two with the loaded comment: 'Catherine told me later that this was the first time they had been alone together in the house' (p. 43).

② The audience sees the strength of feeling between Catherine and Rodolfo in a tender, loving scene.

③ Rodolfo assures Catherine that his feelings for her are genuine despite Eddie's attempt to create doubt in her mind.

④ Rodolfo attempts to persuade her to break away from Eddie, but Catherine shows her reluctance to do so.

⑤ Catherine wants Rodolfo to make love to her and he guides her gently to the bedroom. We see that their relationship is more fulfilling than that between Beatrice and Eddie.

⑥ When Eddie enters unexpectedly, he is drunk and his anger rises when he sees what is happening between Catherine and Rodolfo.

⑦ Eddie orders Rodolfo to go; Catherine attempts to leave. Eddie grabs her and kisses her and when Rodolfo protests, he kisses him also. Catherine says she will kill him.

⑧ When Eddie says, 'Don't make me do nuttin', Catherine' (p. 48), the lovers are left in no doubt that they will be powerless if Eddie decides to act.

WHY IS THIS SECTION IMPORTANT?

A The **strength** of Catherine's and Rodolfo's **relationship** is revealed.

B Miller **builds** the **tension** skilfully as the audience awaits **Eddie's reaction** when he sees **Rodolfo entering from the bedroom** and the full **horror** of the situation strikes him.

C Miller uses two very simple actions, **kissing Catherine** and **kissing Rodolfo**, to show that Eddie has now utterly **overstepped** the bounds of **decency** and become nothing better than a brute.

D Catherine is finally estranged from Eddie when she supports Rodolfo and **threatens** to **kill her uncle**.

E Catherine and Rodolfo realise what **power** Eddie has if he decides to **act**.

THE RELATIONSHIP BETWEEN CATHERINE AND RODOLFO

Up to now we have seen that the two lovers have been happy, enjoying one another's company, exploring the world about them and visiting the various sights of the city. Now, however, Miller enables us to see the strength of their love for one another. They are two very serious young people who want to ensure that they begin their life together on a firm foundation. This is why Catherine wishes to banish any doubts about Rodolfo's reasons for being with her when she asks him about American citizenship.

CHECKPOINT 11

What are Rodolfo's main strengths in this section?

KEY QUOTE

Eddie: 'Don't make me do nuttin', Catherine. Watch your step, submarine. By rights they oughta throw you back in the water.'

Rodolfo is annoyed that the question is raised but he realises that Eddie has created the uncertainty, not Catherine herself. He is aware that if Catherine does not break away from Eddie then she and Rodolfo will not have a life together.

The shocking actions of Eddie when he kisses first Catherine and then Rodolfo shows further evidence of the depth of their love for one another. Rodolfo stands up to him when he says, 'Don't … Stop that! Have respect for her!' (p. 47) and then Catherine screams at him: 'Eddie! Let go, ya hear me! I'll kill you! Leggo of him!' (p. 47). Already we can see that the love between Catherine and Rodolfo is much stronger than that of Eddie and Beatrice, and how it is taking over from Catherine's affection for Eddie.

THE CATALYST

Ever since Rodolfo has arrived at the apartment this moment has been coming. Eddie has been relentless in his dislike for the young man and for his closeness to Catherine.

As an audience we have been expecting it and when it comes it is sharp and sudden. When Eddie sees Rodolfo in the doorway of the bedroom he merely says: 'Pack it up. Go ahead. Get your stuff and get outa here' (p. 47).

DID YOU KNOW

Arthur Miller's play *After the Fall* is a reflection on his marriage to Marilyn Monroe.

EXAMINER'S TIP: WRITING ABOUT MILLER'S DRAMATIC TECHNIQUE

When commenting on Miller's dramatic technique be aware of the way he builds logically to every important moment. This enables the audience to believe in the realism of each situation. Even though we may be surprised by what Eddie does, we know that he is capable of it because of all that has happened before.

Act Two, Part 2: Alfieri sees that Eddie has lost control (pp. 48–9)

SUMMARY

1. Alfieri recognises the terrible change that has come over Eddie and his emptiness of spirit.

2. Alfieri knows, because of the inevitability of the tragedy that is about to happen, that he should do something to prevent it but he feels powerless to do so.

3. Eddie asks for the lawyer's help.

4. Once again the lawyer tells Eddie that no law has been broken and there is nothing he can do.

5. Eddie must, Alfieri says, accept the situation as it is and let nature take its course. If not, Alfieri insists, then everyone will hate him.

6. As Alfieri follows Eddie out, calling to him, the lawyer realises what Eddie is about to do.

WHY IS THIS SECTION IMPORTANT?

A   Alfieri is aware of his own **powerlessness** in a situation like this.

B   We see that Eddie has completely **changed** the atmosphere. None of the action in this section takes place in the Carbones' home.

C   Much as the **audience** may despise what Eddie has done to Catherine and Rodolfo, Miller creates some **sympathy** for him when Eddie says, helplessly, 'So what do I gotta do now? Tell me what to do' (p. 49). This is the **cry of a desperate man**.

D   When Alfieri says, 'Put it out of your mind! Eddie!' (p. 49) we realise that the **inevitable catastrophe** is about to occur.

ALFIERI'S FUNCTION

From now to the end of the play, Alfieri's function is equally divided between being the narrator who interprets the action for the audience and a real character in the play. As a character, he relates to Eddie and attempts to prevent him destroying himself but as a narrator he tells the audience that he knows he is powerless to do so. It is important you can see the difference and how the narrator and the character affects the audience in their own way.

Alfieri also performs the role of the Chorus from Greek tragedy. The Chorus interrupts the action to comment on events and the role of fate. Alfieri's sense of powerlessness in the face of events is an echo of the role of fate in controlling the characters in Greek drama.

? DID YOU KNOW

A View from the Bridge has been, and still is, performed all over the world. It is performed in the US, in the UK and all over Europe, Asia and Australia.

CHECKPOINT 12

How would you describe Beatrice's role in Act Two?

KEY QUOTE

Alfieri: 'Even those who understand will turn against you.'

CHECKPOINT 13

What does Alfieri mean when he says, 'Logically and legally you have no rights' (p. 49)?

KEY QUOTE

Alfieri: 'But I will never forget how dark the room became when he looked at me; his eyes were like tunnels.'

E<small>XAMINER'S</small> <small>TIP</small>: W<small>RITING ABOUT THE USE OF</small> <small>LANGUAGE</small>

You should be prepared to write about the way Arthur Miller uses language in Alfieri's speech. Miller wants to show how helpless Alfieri feels when faced with Eddie's behaviour. Alfieri says that it all felt like being in 'a dream' and that he was 'almost transfixed'. He tells the audience, 'I had lost my strength somewhere' (p. 48).

He talks about the darkness in the room when Eddie looked at him. He states that there was something ghostly about Eddie's eyes, 'which were like tunnels' (p. 48). Miller's use of figurative language here helps to create a gothic-like atmosphere.

DID YOU KNOW

Arthur Miller was arrested and fined because he would not inform on his friends who were communist sympathisers.

Act Two, Part 3: Eddie betrays Marco and Rodolfo (pp. 50–8)

SUMMARY

① Eddie phones the Immigration Bureau and tells the officer that he wishes to report two illegal immigrants.

② Eddie returns home to discover Beatrice on her own. Marco and Rodolfo have moved upstairs to rented accommodation and Catherine is with them.

③ Beatrice tells Eddie that Catherine and Rodolfo are going to be married next week because of fears that Rodolfo might be arrested.

④ Catherine comes down and tells Eddie she is marrying Rodolfo and there is no way he can stop what is about to happen.

⑤ Eddie is distraught when he hears that Marco and Rodolfo are sharing with two other illegal immigrants upstairs.

⑥ Eddie tries to persuade Beatrice to get the men out of the house. He is worried about what their families might do to him if the immigrants are arrested.

⑦ When they arrive, the Immigration Officers are direct and uncompromising. Catherine and Beatrice realise what Eddie has done.

⑧ The four immigrants are led out of the house. Marco spits in Eddie's face. Eddie then threatens to kill Marco. The neighbours turn away from Eddie as he protests his innocence.

WHY IS THIS SECTION IMPORTANT?

A We see Eddie's act of **betrayal** and witness the terrible **irony** of his actions.

B **Catherine's independence** has been established and Eddie no longer has any **power** over her.

C Eddie realises the **consequences** of his **betrayal**. Not only will Marco and Rodolfo be **deported** but **other** illegal immigrants will be **arrested** too.

D Catherine and Beatrice are aware of the **enormity** of **Eddie's treachery**.

E Eddie has now become **despised**, just like Vinny Bolzano became an **outcast** after he informed on a member of his family.

CATHERINE SHOWS HER STRENGTH

Despite Eddie's distress, Catherine tells him that the wedding is on Saturday. She makes it clear that he can go to the wedding if he wishes but, even if he doesn't go, she is determined to marry Rodolfo. When Eddie tries to backtrack, to offer her a way out, she says simply, 'No, we made it up already'. He says, 'But you never knew no other fella, Katie! How could you make up your mind?', but she is not prepared to listen to any argument he can offer. She replies, ''Cause I did. I don't want nobody else' (p. 53). Eddie's actions earlier have made it easy for Catherine to ignore any entreaty from him. Her former warmth and affection have changed to coldness and hostility. When she is with him, Catherine is almost unrecognisable from the person we know from the beginning of the play. Later the audience can

CHECKPOINT 14

Why is it ironic that Eddie is the one who informs on Marco and Rodolfo?

CHECKPOINT 15

How does Eddie react when he discovers that Lipari's nephew is in the house?

KEY QUOTE

Catherine: 'I'm gonna get married, Eddie. If you wanna come, the wedding will be on Saturday.'

see how she tries to defend Rodolfo when the Immigration Officers arrive. She tries to protect him both physically and verbally.

LOSS OF RESPECT

Arthur Miller shows the audience how Eddie has lost the respect of those near to him. When Beatrice discovers his betrayal she says simply, 'My God, what did you do?' (p. 56). The most significant point is made by Marco when he runs into the room and confronts Eddie. He delivers the ultimate insult when he spits in his face. This action is all the more momentous because it is carried out in front of all the neighbours. When Eddie appeals to Lipari to support him, Lipari and his wife turn away from him. Even his friends from the shipyards will have nothing to do with him. When we hear Eddie shouting 'He's gonna take that back or I'll kill him' (p. 58) we are aware that nobody is listening to him and he is completely on his own.

EXAMINER'S TIP: WRITING ABOUT DRAMATIC STRUCTURE

Miller has been building up to this moment of betrayal since the beginning of the play where Alfieri spoke about justice and the law. The Vinny Bolzano story has signposted what was to come. The audience may not have expected Eddie to act in this way but now that he has, there is a certain logic to his behaviour.

A very good exercise for you would be to track the signals given by the playwright. In particular you should analyse the way Eddie's behaviour changes and intensifies from the moment Rodolfo enters. You should also write down detailed reasons for the evidence you find. In terms of dramatic structure, you could say that the play has been building to this climax from the start and from this point it is all down hill for Eddie.

Act Two, Part 4: Marco agrees not to take revenge (pp. 58–60)

SUMMARY

1. While waiting in the reception room of the prison Alfieri asks for Marco's assurance that he will not attack Eddie.

2. Marco finds it difficult to agree because he feels Eddie should be made to pay for what he has done.

3. Catherine and Rodolfo urge him to agree because they want him at their wedding.

4. Catherine condemns Eddie as she pleads with Marco not to do anything he will regret.

5. Alfieri again insists that Marco must not take revenge because it is against the law.

6. Marco is appealing to a justice that is above and beyond the law.

7. Alfieri points out that it is only God who delivers ultimate justice. He argues that Marco can at least work for six weeks before the trial.

8. Marco finally agrees.

GRADE BOOSTER

It is important that you analyse every piece of dialogue spoken by Marco and ask yourself what the consequences might be if Alfieri were not present.

WHY IS THIS SECTION IMPORTANT?

A Again we see Alfieri's role as **mediator** as he attempts to **prevent bloodshed**.

B **Tension** is **building** steadily, enhanced by **Eddie's absence**.

C The **clash between justice and the law** is highlighted. Alfieri is the voice of the law but Marco cannot see any possibilities of achieving justice if he obeys the law.

D There is more evidence of **Catherine's contempt** for **Eddie** when she says, 'To hell with Eddie. Nobody is gonna talk to him again if he lives to a hundred' (p. 59).

E Alfieri's final comment, 'Only God, Marco' (p. 59), implies that even he, as a lawyer, accepts the **limits of the law** and the futility of not settling for half.

BUILDING TENSION

Eddie is not present in this section but, nevertheless, he is never far from our thoughts because everything here is as a direct result of Eddie's actions. In some ways, his absence is even more powerful because Miller forces us to imagine what Eddie's reaction will be when he meets Marco and Rodolfo again.

HONOUR AND JUSTICE

The audience will also be aware that even though Alfieri seems to have extracted a promise from Marco (that he will not do anything to hurt Eddie) that promise is very fragile and can be broken at anytime. When Alfieri says, 'To promise not to kill is not dishonourable' Marco replies: 'No?' (p. 59). That 'No' with a question mark shows how confused Marco is about the law in America. He cannot understand how it can possibly be just.

CHECKPOINT 19

Why is Marco so confused when Alfieri tells him that if Eddie obeys the law he will not be punished?

KEY QUOTE

Marco: 'The law? All the law is not in a book.'

★ GRADE BOOSTER

Read the stage directions here very carefully. When Marco pulls his hand away this is a simple instruction to the director but it is also very important because it tells the audience about Marco's resentment. Look, too, at the direction, *'Alfieri with a certain processional tread leaves the stage'*. What is the significance of this? Make a list of all the important stage directions made by Miller here.

EXAMINER'S TIP: WRITING ABOUT ALFIERI THE CHARACTER

Look carefully at Alfieri's role in this section. Miller has dispensed with Alfieri the narrator for the moment. Instead, the audience see him as a character who is involved in the lives of Marco, Catherine and Rodolfo. Alfieri's, as usual, is the voice of reason and when he speaks to Marco he tries to make him see that the law, while it may seem unjust, must be obeyed.

The implication behind the comment 'Only God makes justice' (p. 60) is that Alfieri feels that often the law is inadequate but, as human beings, we have to abide by the rules set out by the government of the country. Alfieri can see clearly the conflict between justice and the law but he has to insist that Marco does not attack Eddie if only for his own sake.

However, despite his insistence that the law is insurmountable, the audience will feel sympathy for Alfieri during his exchange with Marco when the Italian denounces Eddie. Alfieri feels helpless in the face of Marco's onslaught probably because he empathises with him. Even though Miller does not describe Alfieri's sadness and frustration we sense that both are present. Reading between the lines is very important when you are working towards achieving high grades.

Act Two, Part 5: Eddie's death (pp. 60–4)

SUMMARY

① Beatrice prepares to attend the wedding. Eddie tells her if she goes she must not come back to him.

② Catherine verbally attacks Eddie, calling him a rat that bites people when they sleep.

③ Beatrice tells Catherine she cannot go to her wedding because if she did she would be betraying Eddie.

④ Rodolfo tells Eddie that Marco is praying in the church before coming for him. Eddie says he expects Marco to apologise to him and that he wants respect.

⑤ When Marco enters, Eddie calls on him to apologise for taking away his name. Eddie forces the issue until he has created a confrontation from which Marco cannot withdraw.

⑥ Marco calls Eddie an animal. Eddie lunges at Marco who strikes him and he falls.

⑦ As Marco raises his foot, Eddie draws a knife and lunges again. Marco turns the knife and stabs Eddie.

⑧ Eddie's capacity for self-delusion continues even as he is dying in Beatrice's arms. He says he has been wronged by Catherine and, therefore, by Rodolfo, Marco and even Beatrice. He dies.

⑨ Alfieri concludes by saying it is better to settle for less than the whole truth. While Alfieri believes this, he says he still loves Eddie because he allowed people to see him as he was – completely.

CHECKPOINT 20

What does Eddie mean when he says 'I want my name, Marco' (p. 62)?

WHY IS THIS SECTION IMPORTANT?

A We see that Beatrice **will not betray** Eddie by going to Catherine's wedding.

B Catherine's **vicious attack** on Eddie strips away any possibility he might become **reasonable** again.

C It seems quite likely that Eddie is creating the **inevitable confrontation** because he cannot see any way of walking away from this **betrayal**.

D The audience is invited by the playwright to answer the question: does Eddie really believe that he is the **victim** or is he desperately trying to **cover for his actions**?

E Alfieri's final lines take the audience back to what he was saying in his opening speech about **justice** and its **importance** to the people of Red Hook and Sicily.

CHECKPOINT 21

Why does Beatrice refuse to go to the wedding?

★ GRADE BOOSTER

Whom do you feel most empathy with, Eddie or Marco? You must find good reasons for your answer.

FACING THE TRUTH?

At last Beatrice realises that the truth about Eddie's feelings for Catherine must be confronted. She says, 'You want somethin' else, Eddie, and you can never have her!' In some ways this is comparable to a volcano that has been rumbling under the surface for years and now explodes. Beatrice drives on without pity because she knows that if it is not said now it may lie dormant for ever. She continues, 'The truth is not as bad as blood, Eddie! I'm tellin' you the truth – tell her goodbye forever!' (p. 62).

As an audience we can never be absolutely sure that Eddie realises he has feelings for Catherine other than the totally legitimate ones of an uncle for his niece. He will not accept that the accusation has any truth in it and turns instead to face the challenge of Marco. This is simple. This he can deal with and, of course, he does.

Closing words

Alfieri closes the play with a speech to the audience which tells us that he cannot help but be impressed by a man who would not compromise, 'he allowed himself to be wholly known'. He knows that it is better to 'settle for half' (p. 64) but he is not totally convinced that this is the right way to live. His final line shows the contradictory nature of his feelings for Eddie: 'And so I mourn him – I admit it – with a certain … alarm' (p. 64). He doesn't condemn Eddie. In some ways he admires him. However, he is filled with apprehension now that he has admitted this.

Examiner's tip: Writing about different kinds of justice

Eddie and Marco are both seeking justice in their own ways. Both feel they have been wronged by the other and, because of Alfieri's comments, they realise that they have no recourse to the law. Eddie says to Beatrice, 'He's gonna come here and apologise to me or nobody from this house is goin' into that church today' (p. 60). Earlier Marco has said something similar. So we can see the power of Miller's technique here. The antagonists are being brought ever closer.

The tension builds mainly through the dialogue employed by the other three characters until the climax is reached. Miller was aware that the play could have ended in a number of different ways but whatever transpired the result would have to be tragic for Eddie. It is inconceivable that he could live a normal life after this.

EXAMINER'S TIP

Analyse the three stages of Catherine's behaviour in this section. She is hostile towards Eddie, she pleads with him and finally she asks for his forgiveness when she says, 'Eddie, I never meant to do nothing bad to you!' (p. 64).

KEY QUOTE

Beatrice: 'Whatever happened we all done it, and don't you ever forget it, Catherine.'

CHECKPOINT 22

What does Alfieri mean when he says that Eddie *'allowed himself to be wholly known'* (p. 64)?

Progress and revision check

REVISION ACTIVITY

❶ Why does Eddie encourage Beatrice to tell Catherine the story about Vinny Bolzano? (Write your answers below).

....

❷ Why does Eddie dislike Rodolfo?

....

❸ Why does Marco show his physical superiority over Eddie at the end of Act One?

....

❹ Why does Eddie inform the authorities about Marco and Rodolfo?

....

❺ What motivates Eddie to confront Marco at the end of the play?

....

REVISION ACTIVITY

On a piece of paper, write down answers to these questions:

● What signs are we given in Act One that Eddie's relationship with Catherine is unconventional?

Start: *At the beginning of the play we can see that Eddie's obsessive nature is smothering Catherine because ...*

● How does the playwright create the possibility that there will be a tragic ending?

Start: *During the first Act we are aware of a growing hostility and tension because ...*

GRADE BOOSTER

Answer this longer, practice question about the plot/action of the play:

Q: Do you agree that this is a play about an ordinary man struggling with ordinary problems that he can no longer solve? Think about ...

● The way Eddie is seen as a man who is not very intelligent and who follows his instinct rather than any logical thought process.

● The way his relationship with Catherine leads to conflict and confrontation.

● The fact that Eddie is incapable of accepting any advice.

For a C grade: You must show clear understanding of the effects achieved by the playwright; provide relevant evidence to support your comments about Eddie.

For an A grade: Make sure that you do all of the above, but also focus on specific words and phrases and develop ideas about Eddie from them. You should respond in an original way to the task and to the play. Quotations should be embedded into your comments.

Beatrice

WHO IS BEATRICE?

Beatrice is Eddie's wife and Catherine's aunt by marriage.
She is related to Marco and Rodolfo, the illegal immigrants.

WHAT DOES BEATRICE DO IN THE PLAY?

- Beatrice is loving and caring throughout.

- She is often the mediator when Eddie's aggressiveness creates hostile situations.

- She warns Eddie that the relationship with Catherine is not within acceptable boundaries.

- She is prepared to make sacrifices to help restore sanity – she refuses to attend Catherine's wedding because Eddie does not want her to go.

- At the end she is there to comfort Eddie as he is about to die.

HOW IS BEATRICE'S CHARACTER REVEALED?

Quotation	Means?
(*She turns and grabs Eddie's face in her hands.*) 'Mmm! You're an angel! God'll bless you.' (p. 8)	Beatrice is a warm-hearted person. She shows gratitude whenever anyone helps her or her family.
'I know, honey. But if you act like a baby and he be treatin' you like a baby. Like when he comes home sometimes you throw yourself at him like when you was twelve years old.' (p. 30)	Beatrice is keenly aware of the dangers involved in the relationship between Catherine and Eddie and tries to warn Catherine gently. We see her sensitivity and also her instinct for problems that lurk beneath the surface.
'No, she wants to ask you. Come on, Katie, ask him. We'll have a party!' (p. 53)	Beatrice acts as the mediator.
He [Eddie] dies in her arms, and Beatrice covers him with her body. (p. 64)	Despite all that Eddie has done to destroy their lives Beatrice, as always, shows her unconditional love for him.

EXAMINER'S TIP: WRITING ABOUT BEATRICE

Remember that Beatrice is always thinking about the welfare of others. Even when she speaks forcefully to Eddie she is doing so to help him as well as Catherine. In the end, like Alfieri, she is powerless to prevent Eddie acting in his destructive way but she is, nevertheless, faithful to him.

GRADE BOOSTER

Make a list of Beatrice's qualities throughout the play and find an example for each. For instance: Beatrice is protective and maternal as shown in the way she helps Catherine break the news of her job to Eddie.

DID YOU KNOW

A View from the Bridge began life as a one act play in the form of a Greek tragedy.

Eddie

WHO IS EDDIE?

Eddie Carbone is a longshoreman whose job it is to load and unload boats in the shipyards of Brooklyn.

WHAT DOES EDDIE DO IN THE PLAY?

- Eddie is protective towards Catherine. Soon this protectiveness becomes obsessive and unnatural.

- Even though he can be warm and generous, there are few moments in the play when he is not in conflict with the other characters.

- Eddie's jealousy of Rodolfo shows how emotionally unstable he is.

- He breaks his code of honour by betraying Rodolfo and Marco when it seems his relationship with Catherine is threatened.

- He loses the respect of all who know him and therefore has no option but to face Marco in mortal combat.

- In the end he gains some dignity in the manner of his death.

HOW IS EDDIE'S CHARACTER REVEALED?

Quotation	Means?
'I don't understand you; she's seventeen years old, you gonna keep her in the house all her life?' (p. 11)	This comment from Beatrice to Eddie tells the audience that he is too protective, too possessive of Catherine and he should be able to see that she is old enough to look after herself.
'I take the blankets off my bed for him, and he takes and puts his filthy hands on her like a goddam thief!' (p. 35)	Eddie's reaction to Rodolfo demonstrates how emotionally unstable and irrational he is. He cannot see the young man's qualities. Instead he is blinded by his fear that Rodolfo will take Catherine away from him.
'He was good to me, Rodolfo. You don't know him; he was always the sweetest guy to me.' (p. 45)	Catherine sees the positive side of Eddie. He is obviously capable of much warmth and generosity and she really appreciates this – at least for now. But she is also speaking in the past tense almost as if he was a different person then.
'Give me the number of the Immigration Bureau. I want to report something. Illegal immigrants.' (p. 50)	Self-interest is one of Eddie's great motivating factors. He is deeply aware of the horrific nature of betraying an immigrant to the authorities and yet, when his own comfortable relationship with Catherine comes under threat, he is quite prepared to break this code of honour.

GRADE BOOSTER

When thinking about Eddie find a new quotation for each of the following characteristics:
1) forceful;
2) obsessive;
3) warm;
4) protective;
5) irrational.
Now write what you think each quotation really means.

GRADE BOOSTER

Read all the comments made by Alfieri and Beatrice about Eddie. Write all the positive and negative remarks made by both characters and then write a few sentences saying what each observation tells the audience about Eddie and the characters' attitude to him at that time.

Examiner's tip: Writing about Eddie

Think about the way Miller creates the character of Eddie. At the beginning he seems to be a strong family man with a sense of humour. We also see him as a protective uncle who looks out for his niece, Catherine.

You could then move on to write about the way his character changes when Rodolfo arrives. Show how his protective nature shifts to obsession. Miller, at the beginning of Act Two, shows how unpleasant Eddie can be when he is angry. Try discussing the reasons for Eddie's actions when he breaks the community code that demands that illegal immigrants are protected from the law. Finally analyse the tragic consequences of Eddie's betrayal and discuss whether he deliberately engineers his own death because of his shame.

You should consider the gradual disintegration of the character until, in the end, all Eddie's positive qualities have disappeared and he is a shell of the man we saw at the beginning of the play. Don't forget to quote at appropriate intervals to support your comments.

EXAMINER'S TIP

It is important that you explain what the characters say, what they don't say, what they do and what they don't do. You should also analyse the situation each character finds himself or herself in. All this will help you to understand the dramatic overall purpose.

Catherine

WHO IS CATHERINE?

Catherine is Eddie's niece. She is seventeen years old. She is a pleasant, attractive character. She can be very strong when necessary.

EXAMINER'S TIP

When writing about characters in a play it is advantageous to show how others see them. Beatrice loves Catherine but she finds her naïve and advises her accordingly. It is also worthwhile looking at the way Eddie and Rodolfo see her.

WHAT DOES CATHERINE DO IN THE PLAY?

- Catherine is about to start her first job despite Eddie's objections.

- When Rodolfo arrives she is attracted to him and begins a very intense relationship with him which will lead to marriage.

- Eddie creates doubts about Rodolfo's motives but Catherine accepts Rodolfo's assurance that he is genuine in his attentions.

- She shows her strength of character when she takes sides against Eddie and is vehement in her condemnation of him.

- However, at the end of the play, she murmurs her heartfelt regret for her part in Eddie's tragic end.

HOW IS CATHERINE'S CHARACTER REVEALED?

GRADE BOOSTER

Find three more quotes to show how Catherine changes her attitude towards Eddie during the play. Give reasons for your choices and explain each quote in detail.

Quotation	Means?
'She's crazy to start work. It's not a little shop, it's a big company. Some day she could be a secretary. They picked her out of the whole class.' (p. 10)	Catherine is desperate to be independent. She is obviously well thought of at her college. However, we can see that Eddie has control over her.
Catherine (*flushed with revolt*): 'You wanna dance, Rodolfo?' (*Eddie freezes*). (p. 39)	Now that Rodolfo has arrived Catherine has the strength to show her independence despite Eddie's discomfort.
Catherine (*clearing from Beatrice*): 'What're you scared of? He's a rat! He belongs in the sewer.' (p. 61)	Eddie has betrayed Marco and Rodolfo, and Catherine's love and respect for him have turned to hate and loathing. She feels sufficiently strong to tell him this to his face.
The two women support him for a moment calling his name again and again. Catherine: 'Eddie, I never meant to do nothing bad to you.' (p. 64)	In the end, Catherine feels guilty for all that has happened. She had no idea it could end so tragically.

DID YOU KNOW

The Arthur Miller Society is devoted to the study of the playwright's works. The website is updated on a weekly basis.

EXAMINER'S TIP: WRITING ABOUT CATHERINE

Catherine is the most likeable figure in the play. Her relationship with Eddie and Beatrice through most of Act One is warm and friendly. She is excited about the arrival of the immigrants and when they enter she is entranced by them, especially by Rodolfo. You should be aware of the gradual change in Catherine while at the same time acknowledging her fondness for Eddie. It isn't until the beginning of Act Two that Catherine shows outright hostility towards him after he kisses first her and then Rodolfo in a drunken rage. Of course, the final shocking act is the betrayal which forces Catherine to cut all ties with her uncle.

Marco

WHO IS MARCO?

Marco is an illegal immigrant who has arrived from Sicily. He is married with three young children. He is the older of the two brothers and feels responsible for Rodolfo.

WHAT DOES MARCO DO IN THE PLAY?

- Marco has come to America because he needs to support his wife and family.

- He has a strong sense of right and wrong and when Eddie hits Rodolfo he is ready to protect his younger brother.

- When he discovers that Eddie has betrayed him he feels he has the right to take revenge.

- When speaking to Alfieri he does not understand why the law will allow Eddie to go free.

- Marco kills Eddie by turning Eddie's own knife on him.

- We do not know if Marco would have killed Eddie if Eddie had not pulled a knife. However, Marco does not show regret.

HOW IS MARCO'S CHARACTER REVEALED?

Quotation	Means?
Stage direction: *(he is a square-built peasant of thirty-two, suspicious, tender, and quiet-voiced).* (p. 16)	Physically, Marco is very strong. He is wary of those around him and does not trust people until he knows them. He loves his brother and his family back in Sicily.
Stage direction: *Marco is face to face with Eddie, a strained tension gripping his eyes and jaw ...* (p. 42)	Marco's sense of fair play forces him to act in defence of his brother. Without actually threatening Eddie he makes it clear that Eddie will be in trouble if he hurts Rodolfo.

EXAMINER'S TIP

Even though Marco says and does less than any of the other main characters, his actions are very significant and create big dramatic moments. Find two more quotes which show Marco's actions or words are of great importance.

GRADE BOOSTER

Marco's attitude to justice and the law is seen most clearly in the section p. 58 to p. 60, where he speaks to Alfieri. Read through this section and write notes about Marco's comments to Alfieri.

EXAMINER'S TIP

Showing that you feel empathy with a character is important if you hope to achieve high grades. As an exercise you should write about the empathy you feel (or don't feel) for Marco. You would, of course, have to give very good reasons for your answer.

Quotation	Means?
Stage direction: *Marco suddenly breaks from the group and dashes into the room and faces Eddie; Beatrice and First Officer rush in as Marco spits into Eddie's face.* (pp. 56–7)	Marco's outrage is so great that he loses all control. He cannot understand how one human being would do this to another. Spitting in Eddie's face shows his utter contempt for him.
'The law? All the law is not in a book.' (p. 59)	Marco believes it is his duty to right this wrong without recourse to the law. He believes that the law has nothing to do with his need for justice.

EXAMINER'S TIP: WRITING ABOUT MARCO

Marco is the strong silent type until he believes that an injustice has taken place. He is totally unselfish. Unlike Rodolfo he has not come to America for adventure or to fulfil his dream. Instead he has come to support his family and will go home as soon as possible. He is hugely grateful to Beatrice and Eddie for allowing him and Rodolfo to stay. At the beginning he supports Eddie's attempts to control Rodolfo's exuberance because he believes Eddie is doing this for the right reasons. Important though the character is, he is the one we know least about.

Rodolfo

Find a number of comments made by Eddie about Rodolfo which are meant to show him in a negative way. How would you respond to these comments? Do they say more about Eddie than they do about Rodolfo?

WHO IS RODOLFO?

Rodolfo is Marco's younger brother. Unlike Marco, he would be happy to become an American citizen and settle down in the country. He is an attractive young man with a lively sense of humour.

WHAT DOES RODOLFO DO IN THE PLAY?

● Rodolfo makes an immediate and very positive impact as soon as he enters.

● He is a man of many talents. He can cook, he can sing and he can make clothes.

● Catherine falls in love with him very quickly and, in return, Rodolfo's love for her is genuine and powerful.

● Eddie dislikes Rodolfo because he knows that he will take Catherine away from him.

● Towards the end of the play, Rodolfo is the one who is aware of the terrible consequences of the battle of wills between Eddie and Marco.

● He tries to keep the peace by apologising to Eddie even though he does not need to say sorry.

HOW IS RODOLFO'S CHARACTER REVEALED?

Quotation	Means?
'Oh, I sing Napolidan, jazz, bel canto – I sing "Paper Doll".' (p. 21)	We are given a flavour of Rodolfo's many talents.
Catherine: 'Teach me.' (*She is weeping*) 'I don't know anything, teach me, Rodolfo, hold me.' (p. 46)	Rodolfo is capable of inspiring trust and love. He is an open, warm hearted character.
'I would like to go to Broadway once, Eddie. I would like to walk with her once where theatres are and the opera.' (p. 26)	Rodolfo shows his sense of wonder and adventure. He wants new experiences.
'It is my fault, Eddie. Everything. I wish to apologise. It was wrong that I did not ask your permission.' (p. 62)	Rodolfo, the peacemaker, is prepared to accept responsibility for a situation that is not of his making. He will go to great lengths to prevent the approaching tragedy.

EXAMINER'S TIP: WRITING ABOUT RODOLFO

Miller has created a very attractive character in Rodolfo. He loves life. He is irrepressible and this quality has a positive effect on most people he meets. However, he also has a serious, thoughtful side to him which shows he is sensitive to those around him. It is easy to see why Catherine falls in love with him. She has never met such a talented, responsive young man before and against a background of the ordinary, unimaginative people she usually meets she is easily swept off her feet.

Alfieri

WHO IS ALFIERI?

Alfieri is a narrator, commentator and also a character in the play. He is a lawyer and is thus removed from the other characters. More than anybody else in the play he can see the coming tragedy.

WHAT DOES ALFIERI DO IN THE PLAY?

- Alfieri attempts to place the events of the drama in context and explain to the audience that conflicts such as these occur throughout Italian history.

- His role is to oversee the action and attempt to remain objective throughout. However, at the end, he does have sympathy for Eddie and even some admiration for him.

KEY QUOTE

Eddie: 'Mr Alfieri, they're laughin' at him on the piers. I'm ashamed. Paper Doll they call him. Blondie now. His brother thinks it's because he's got a sense of humour, see – which he's got – but that ain't what they're laughin'.'

GRADE BOOSTER

Find three more examples of Rodolfo's dialogue which show him to be a lively, outgoing personality who is very engaging.

EXAMINER'S TIP

Make sure that you realise when Alfieri is (a) being a commentator, (b) being a narrator and (c) being a character. It might help you if you wrote notes about him under these three headings.

KEY QUOTE

Alfieri: 'Now we settle for half, and I like it better. I no longer keep a pistol in my filing cabinet.'

- Alfieri knows it is better to 'settle for half' (p. 64) because sometimes the search for absolute justice results in unacceptable consequences.

- As the audience prepare to leave the theatre he offers some universal concepts for them to think about.

HOW IS ALFIERI'S CHARACTER REVEALED?

Quotation	Means?
'I am inclined to notice the ruins in things perhaps because I was born in Italy … I only came here when I was twenty-five.' (p. 4)	Alfieri is of Italian extraction and is therefore in a position to empathise with the other characters.
'And I sat there many afternoons asking myself why, being an intelligent man, I was so powerless to stop it.' (p. 35)	We see Alfieri as the on-looker, who can interpret what is happening and how it is going to end, feeling utterly frustrated because he cannot prevent the inevitable tragedy. He performs the role of the Greek Chorus, commenting on events but unable to change them.
'You won't have a friend in the world, Eddie! Even those who understand will turn against you …' (p. 49)	Even though Eddie has not declared his intention to betray the brothers Alfieri is aware that he is going to do so. He is desperate to stop him.
'This is not God, Marco. You hear? Only God makes justice.' (p. 60)	Alfieri has been trying to tell Marco, as previously he told Eddie, that the law does not always deliver justice. Sometimes, he says, we have to rely on God.

EXAMINER'S TIP: WRITING ABOUT ALFIERI

It is worth noting that Alfieri's main function is to help the audience make sense of what is happening on stage. He usually knows what is about to happen before any of the other characters. However, as a character in the play, he has very little influence over the others. Thus, for example, he is ineffectual when he tries to prevent Eddie and later Marco from behaving in a catastrophic way. His message that it is better to 'settle for half' (p. 64) is repeated throughout the play in the way he talks to Eddie and Marco, trying to persuade them to behave in a reasonable manner.

Progress and revision check

REVISION ACTIVITY

❶ How would you describe Eddie's character? (Write your answers below)

....

❷ How does Eddie feel about Catherine?

....

❸ Who has more impact on the play: Marco or Rodolfo?

....

❹ How does Beatrice try to stabilise the situation when Eddie appears to be ready to self-destruct?

....

❺ How does Catherine's attitude towards Eddie change as the play develops?

....

REVISION ACTIVITY

On a piece of paper, write down answers to these questions.

● Choose a character whom you like or dislike and follow their progress in the drama.

Start: *I particularly like the character of Rodolfo because of his approach to life ...*

● Discuss the character of Catherine. Why is she important to the story of the play?

Start: *Catherine is an important character in the play because of the way she confronts Eddie ...*

GRADE BOOSTER

Answer this longer, practice question about the characters of the play:

Q. Examine the characters of Rodolfo and Catherine. Explore their relationship as it changes and develops through the play. Think about ...

● How Catherine views Rodolfo when first they meet.
● The way Rodolfo's behaviour attracts Catherine.
● How Catherine's attitude towards Eddie changes as a result of her relationship with Rodolfo.
● Catherine's determination to marry Rodolfo despite Eddie's opposition.

For a C grade: Make sure that you use all the relevant facts to show that you clearly understand the characters and what motivates them.

For an A grade: Make sure that you do all of the above, but also chose relevant quotations to support what you say. Refer to specific examples to show that you can analyse the playwright's technique and can explore ideas and attitudes.

Key contexts

THE AUTHOR: ARTHUR MILLER

Arthur Miller was born on 17 October 1915 in New York. In 1934 he enrolled at the University of Michigan. While there he was awarded prizes for playwriting. He graduated in English in 1938.

His first success was the play *All My Sons,* which was produced in 1947. The play won two Tony awards. His greatest success, however, was *Death of a Salesman* which brought him international fame and the Pulitzer Prize. His other major plays were *A View from the Bridge* and *The Crucible*.

He married the film star Marilyn Monroe in 1956, but the marriage only lasted for five years.

A View from the Bridge was completed in 1956. It was the playwright's last major success. He died of heart failure at the age of eighty-nine in 2005. He is widely regarded as one of the greatest playwrights of the twentieth century.

PERSONAL EXPERIENCES

In the 1940s Arthur Miller spent two years working with Italians in the shipyards of Brooklyn and was thus able to study the social background of the lives of the longshoremen (dock workers) in that area. Much of the experience and knowledge he gleaned from this time served as raw material for *A View from the Bridge*. It was during this time that the playwright heard the story of a longshoreman who had betrayed two of his relatives to the Immigration authorities because he was not happy about the relationship between one of the immigrants and his niece.

As well as having close associations with the families of the dock workers at this time, Arthur Miller gained inspiration for the play from a conversation he had with a friend. In his autobiography *Time Bends* he described how a friend told him about a dream he had about an attraction he felt for his cousin. When Miller interpreted the dream as an indication that the man might have wanted an incestuous relationship with the girl he was horrified (like Eddie) and refused to accept that there might be any truth in what Miller was saying.

SETTING AND PLACE

The play is set in Red Hook in Brooklyn, which is part of New York. Red Hook is a poverty-stricken slum area where the Carbones and their neighbours live. Alfieri, the lawyer, views the drama from Brooklyn Bridge. The bridge is symbolic of the view Alfieri has of the activity that is taking place in Red Hook. It is also a symbol of the avenue between the dreams of the Italian immigrants and America. Most of the action takes place in the Carbones' living room and dining room but some scenes are located in the street outside their house. It is important that we see the Carbones as part of the wider community, especially towards the end of the play when their private tragedy is acted out before the whole neighbourhood.

ORDINARY LIVES

At the time the play is the set, longshoremen were not very well paid even though Marco and Rodolfo think their wages amount to wealth beyond their dreams.

Many of the workers were illegal immigrants and were being exploited by the very people who helped bring them to America. They looked after the immigrants until such time as they had paid for their services and then they were left to fend for themselves. Eddie talks about this to Marco.

Eddie and Beatrice want a quiet, contented life with few problems. As Alfieri says 'Eddie Carbone had never expected to have a destiny. A man works, raises his family, goes bowling, eats, gets old and then he dies' (p. 22). When the illegal immigrants arrive there is little evidence, initially, that the family's comfort will be disturbed. When eventually Eddie's obsession intrudes, neither he nor the others can cope with the turbulence because they have no experience of dealing with problems of this nature.

In his plays, Arthur Miller explores the struggles of the ordinary man against authority and insurmountable odds. His examination of the past, and how it can haunt the present and the future, is a powerful way to dramatise the thin line every person walks through life. While examining and exposing human weakness he also shows an understanding of the deep-lying emotions within every human being.

> **? DID YOU KNOW**
>
> Arthur Miller received a lifetime achievement award when he was eighty-three. As he accepted it he joked to the audience, 'Just being around to collect it is a pleasure.'

EXAMINER'S TIP: WRITING ABOUT BACKGROUND

Make sure that you are aware of the background to the play and how Miller used real events to shape his drama. It is always worthwhile to embed this knowledge into your answer.

Key themes

THE RELATIONSHIP BETWEEN EDDIE AND CATHERINE

At the beginning of the play we are immediately aware that there is a lively, intimate relationship between Catherine and Eddie. There are no barriers. Eddie is delighted at her beauty, but because of this beauty he fears what other men will see. Catherine is unhappy when Eddie objects to her going out to work. Beatrice tells Eddie he is smothering Catherine and stifling her independence.

When the cousins arrive, Eddie is quickly aware of the attraction Rodolfo has for Catherine and from this moment onwards Eddie attempts to place a barrier between them. Like Beatrice, Alfieri is aware of the dangerous nature of the relationship. He also warns Eddie that he must not feel as he does for Catherine.

Every statement made by Alfieri makes it clear that the relationship must end now or it will have tragic consequences. In the end, of course, Catherine's hostile attack on Eddie is a statement that she has now finally broken free from him. The break in the relationship is complete.

REVISION ACTIVITY

Here are some key moments related to this theme. Can you find any others?

- Eddie's pride in Catherine's appearance is obvious when she appears in her new clothes:

  Eddie: 'Beautiful. Turn round, lemme see in the back' (*she turns for him*) 'Oh, if your mother was alive to see you now! She wouldn't believe it' (p. 5).

- Eddie is angry as he waits for Catherine and Rodolfo to return. He is beginning to show how dangerously obsessive he can be:

  Eddie: 'They must've seen every picture in Brooklyn by now. He's supposed to stay in the house when he ain't working. He ain't supposed to go advertising himself' (p. 22).

- Eddie's attitude and behaviour eventually forces Catherine to realise that she has to break away from him:

  Catherine: 'I think I can't stay here no more.' (*She frees her arm, steps back towards the bedroom.*) 'I'm sorry, Eddie.' (*She sees the tears in his eyes.*) 'Well, don't cry. I'll be around the neighbourhood' (p. 47).

- Finally, Catherine is totally disillusioned by Eddie. Her attack on him is uncompromising and destroys any possibility that they can continue any relationship:

  Catherine (*weeping*): He bites people when they sleep! He comes when nobody's lookin' and poisons decent people. In the garbage he belongs!' (*Eddie seems about to pick up the table and fling it at her*) (p. 61).

DID YOU KNOW

Arthur Miller said that, 'the best work anybody ever writes is the work that is on the verge of embarrassing him …'

EXAMINER'S TIP: WRITING ABOUT EDDIE AND CATHERINE

When writing about the significance of the relationship between Eddie and Catherine use evidence from the play. Find two more examples to show aspects of the relationship, write down why they are appropriate and find a quote to support your ideas.

MANLINESS

Eddie may never admit that manliness consists of knowing one's boundaries and protecting one's territory, but that is clearly what he feels. Other men are regarded as hostile invaders if they enter his world.

Eddie does not regard Rodolfo as a real man because he cooks, sings, makes dresses and has platinum hair. He calls him 'Paper Doll' (p. 33) 'Canary' and 'a weird' (p. 23). Beatrice suggests he is jealous of Rodolfo but Eddie rejects this.

Eddie keeps his distance. He does not regard it as manly to show his emotions. His comments and questions have an edge to them which make the other characters uncomfortable. Eddie's own masculinity is called into question when Beatrice asks him, 'When am I gonna be a wife again, Eddie?' (p. 24). Later he tells Beatrice that she must never ask him questions like this again.

Generally speaking, Eddie is a simple man who feels uncomfortable when his manliness is threatened. When he is confused he refuses to accept anything other than his own uncomplicated measure of masculinity.

REVISION ACTIVITY

Here are some key moments related to this theme. Can you think of any others?

- Eddie feels that his position is being weakened when Rodolfo enters his house:

  Eddie: 'I take the blankets off my bed for him, and he takes and puts his filthy hands on her like a goddam thief' (p. 35).

- Eddie believes that if Marco apologises in front of his neighbours for spitting at him he will be a man again:

  Eddie: Marco's got my name – (*to Rodolfo*) and you can run tell him, kid, that he's gonna give it back to me in front of this neighbourhood, or we have it out' (p. 62).

- Eddie imagines that Beatrice is calling his manliness into question and this disturbs him. He is convinced that this should not happen in his house and that Beatrice should respect him:

  Eddie: I want my respect, Beatrice, and you know what I'm talkin' about' (p. 51).

? **DID YOU KNOW**

If Rodolfo marries Catherine, who is an American citizen, he will have the legal right to stay in America.

EXAMINER'S TIP

Apart from the themes explored here you should attempt to search out some for yourself. Read through Alfieri's speeches and you will find a number of ideas that are worth analysis.

Justice and the Law

Alfieri, as a lawyer, is aware that the law, despite its limitations, must be upheld. However, he is also aware of the inability of the law to dispense total justice. He feels powerless to intervene when a character in the play decides to find justice in his own way – outside the law.

Eddie Carbone is a man who does not understand the reasons for the limitations of the law. Early in the play he asks Beatrice to tell Catherine the story of Vinny Bolzano. In Eddie's eyes and in the eyes of the community Vinny was guilty of injustice and his family ensured that justice was done when he was punished and shunned by the neighbourhood. There is a feeling that if people always abide by the law then they will have to 'settle for half' (p. 4). Alfieri seems to be saying that the law is often incapable of satisfying everybody.

Eddie tries to force Alfieri to give him his kind of justice. He believes (or says that he believes) that Rodolfo is going to marry Catherine in order to make him a legal immigrant. He feels that this is unjust and that the law should be capable of making a case against Rodolfo. Alfieri is very rational and unemotional as he informs Eddie that no law has been broken. The real injustice as far as Eddie is concerned is that Rodolfo, who, according to Eddie, is an effeminate 'weird' (p. 23), is taking Catherine for his own and away from Eddie who is, in his own opinion, all that a man should be.

Alfieri warns Eddie that if he betrays the brothers he will be breaching the code of his people and that they will turn against him. Here Alfieri is placing the law against natural justice – he is emphasising that it would be unjust to betray the Italians even if Eddie is actually upholding the law by reporting them.

In the final section of the play Marco demands justice and, as he does so, he echoes the sentiments spoken earlier by Eddie. He says, 'The law? All the law is not in a book' (p. 59). He talks about honour and he talks about blood and about degradation – all of which matter to Marco when he speaks of justice. Again, Alfieri cautions against stepping outside the law.

Throughout the play there is an emphasis on justice, but as Alfieri tells us, there is a price to pay for total justice – a price that most people, most of the time, are not prepared to pay. This is why the majority feel that 'it is better to settle for half' (p. 64).

KEY QUOTE

Eddie: 'I don't care who sees them goin' in and out as long as you don't see them goin' in and out.'

EXAMINER'S TIP

It is very important that you know where justice and the law are discussed in the play. Commit the page numbers to memory. You will then be able to find quotations quickly if necessary.

EXAMINER'S TIP

Produce a single revision sheet for each of the key themes. Set it out in the form of a diagram with essential quotations and some phrases of your own.

Examiner's tip: Writing about betrayal

In the play, Miller stays firmly in the background and allows the audience to decide who is right and who is wrong. It seems that Eddie is well aware that informing on the Italians to the authorities is betrayal but has he been pushed beyond the limits of control by circumstances? Alfieri knows that the law has been broken but not by Eddie. He warns Eddie that he will be ostracised by the community if he makes that phone call. So there are shades of grey here. Think about all the pressures on the characters before you answer a question.

Progress and revision check

REVISION ACTIVITY

1. Why does Eddie react in the way he does when he discovers that Catherine has a job? (Write your answers below)

....

2. What does Alfieri say about Eddie's relationship with Catherine?

....

3. Why does Rodolfo unsettle Eddie?

....

4. Why does Alfieri imply that the law is incapable of satisfying everybody?

....

5. What is the code that Eddie is in danger of breaking according to Alfieri?

....

REVISION ACTIVITY

On a piece of paper, write down answers to these questions:

● Why are law and justice such important themes in the play?

Start: *Law and justice are the most important themes because they form the basis of ...*

● Why is the theme of manliness so significant to Eddie?

Start: *Eddie sees himself as a real man and this is important to him because ...*

GRADE BOOSTER

Answer this longer, practice question about the plot/action of the play:

Q: In what way is Eddie upholding the law and, at the same time, breaking the code of natural justice, when he makes his phone call? Think about ...

● The story of Vinny Bolzano.
● The way Alfieri discusses the law and justice.
● Eddie's advice to Catherine at the beginning about keeping quiet.
● The reason why Eddie did phone the authorities.

For a C grade: You will have to show clear understanding of what is meant by the law and justice especially to Eddie and his neighbours.

For an A grade: Make sure that you do all of the above. Make sure you chose relevant quotations to support what you say. You must refer to specific examples to show how Eddie might feel he had no option but to do this. You must respond in an imaginative way if you hope to achieve the highest mark.

Language

Here are some useful terms to know when studying *A View from the Bridge*, what they mean and how they appear in the play.

Literary term	Means?	Example
Irony	A way of writing in which what is meant is the opposite to what the words express.	Eddie tells the story of Vinny Bolzano to show he believes no-one should betray illegal immigrants, yet he does betray them for his own selfish ends.
Climax	Any point of great intensity in a literary work.	In *A View from the Bridge* the climax is discovered when, at the end of the play, Marco turns the knife on Eddie and kills him.
Colloquialism	The use of expressions and grammar associated with ordinary, everyday speech rather than formal language which Alfieri uses.	The speech of Catherine, Eddie and Beatrice is regarded as colloquial. An example is when Eddie says: 'Him? You'll never see him no more, a guy do a thing like that? How's he gonna show his face?' (p. 14).
Chorus	In the tragedies of the Ancient Greek playwright Aeschylus, the Chorus is a group that represents ordinary people in their attitudes to the action which they witness as bystanders and on which they comment.	Alfieri takes the place of the Greek Chorus as he reacts to the events taking place on stage. Like the Chorus in the Greek drama he is powerless to affect events.
Protagonist	In Greek drama the principal character and actor. Now it is often used to describe the 'hero' referring to the leading character in the play.	Eddie is the protagonist in *A View from the Bridge* though we might argue about the term 'hero' when referring to him.

EXAMINER'S TIP

Knowing what a literary term is and recognising it is all very well but you won't get much credit unless you know why it is being used.

THE LANGUAGE THE CHARACTERS SPEAK

There are a variety of language forms in *A View from the Bridge*. The audience hears the educated, controlled dialogue of Alfieri, the aggressive uneducated speech of Eddie, the intelligent, attractive conversations of Rodolfo, the heavy serious tones of Marco, the lively searching words of Catherine and, finally, the quiet, serious language of Beatrice. Arthur Miller's dialogue is, in turn, powerful, economical, colourful and dramatic.

ALFIERI – EDUCATED, CONTROLLED DIALOGUE

EXAMINER'S TIP

A feature of A Grade writing on literature is the ability to see two possible interpretations and to support a preference for one of them.

● Alfieri's language is thoughtful and helps the audience to think about the issues which Miller feels are important. His leisurely style draws the audience into his story and helps to maintain a relationship with them throughout the play. In the opening lines he uses the pronoun 'you' to indicate he is talking directly to the audience. The use of 'you' also shows that he is the link between the audience and the characters.

● Alfieri's wry sense of humour at the beginning of Act One, when he refers to himself as an object of superstition, and again at the beginning of Act Two when he mentions the case of Scotch whisky slipping 'from a net while being unloaded' (p. 43) endears his audience to him. His way of speaking also shows a detachment from the events taking place which allows the character to take an objective view of the whole proceedings. Because he is also a character in the play, he speaks in a different way when communicating with the other characters. He speaks as a lawyer but he also speaks as a family friend might when giving sound advice.

● There is sometimes a wide sweep to the language used by Alfieri, particularly at the beginning of Act One when he says, 'every few years there is still a case and, as the parties tell me what the trouble is, the flat air in my office suddenly washes in with the green scent of the sea' and he goes on to link this case with another in Italy more than a thousand years before. Using colourful locations, e.g. 'Calabria' and 'Syracuse' (p. 4), he gives the scene an importance and relevance that indicates the events are timeless and no respecters of boundaries.

● There are echoes of this style during Act Two, 'But I will never forget how dark the room became when he looked at me, his eyes were like tunnels' (p. 48) and in the final speech when he focuses on the tragedy that is Eddie's: 'I tremble, for I confess that something perversely pure calls to me from his memory – not purely good, but himself purely, for he allowed himself to be wholly known and for that I think I will love him more than all my sensible clients' (p. 64).

RAW POWER OF EDDIE'S SPEECH

● Eddie's dialogue is in sharp contrast to Alfieri's speech. We observe his limited language skills but even so there is a raw power evident in what he says. He speaks in short, uncomplicated sentences which do not allow him to develop his thoughts.

● His language can often be brutally unpleasant and uncompromising, for example when he orders Rodolfo to leave after he sees him coming out of Catherine's bedroom, and at the end of the play when he accuses Marco of taking away his name.

● Quite often he does not complete words or sentences, and he also runs words together. Even so, he does occasionally express himself in a colourful way, such as when he tells Catherine that she is 'walkin' wavy' and that the men's heads are 'turnin' like windmills' (p. 6).

● His language nearly always betrays a fiercely narrow focus. At the end of the play he keeps on repeating that he wants his name back. The rawness of the language lacks any subtlety and it is this primitive use of words that creates the tension at the end of Act One, the viciousness in the way he tells Rodolfo to leave and, finally, the tragic events at the end of the play.

DIALOGUE

Arthur Miller sometimes uses dialogue to show the lack of communication between the characters. A powerful example of this is when Beatrice accuses Eddie of not being a proper husband to her:

Beatrice:	No, everything ain't great with me.
Eddie:	No?
Beatrice:	No. But I got other worries.
Eddie:	Yeah. (*He is already weakening.*)
Beatrice:	Yeah, you want me to tell you?
Eddie (*in retreat*):	Why? What worries you got? (p. 24)

EXAMINER'S TIP

While stage directions usually contain important information, you should not spend too much time writing about them, because this might distract you from the dialogue.

Eddie is refusing to respond to her probing because he does not want to recognise what he feels for Catherine and his lack of love for Beatrice. He speaks in short bursts which he hopes will prevent further scrutiny. He says, 'No?', 'Yeah', 'Why? What worries you got?'. The last example is not an invitation to speak but a **rhetorical** question to silence her. When Beatrice continues relentlessly he stops the questions with a blunt, 'I don't want to talk about it' and 'I got nothin' to say about it!' (p. 24).

In the final section of Act One Eddie speaks to Rodolfo as if he is complimenting him by comparing Rodolfo's talent with his own lack of skill. He repeats his list of Rodolfo's talents – three times he lists them – superficially to show how much he admires him but in reality he wants Rodolfo to be seen as effeminate and not as a real man. About the coffee that Catherine offers to make he says, 'Make it nice and strong' (p. 40) indicating that he, a real man, likes his coffee strong.

POWER THROUGH ECONOMY

We see the power and economy of Miller's language in the final page of Act One. Marco does not need to tell Eddie that he is the stronger man. His actions (indicated by Miller's stage directions) and his brief invitation to Eddie, 'Can you lift this chair?' (p. 42) are sufficient to create a very intense moment which speaks volumes about the change of **atmosphere** and the change in the way characters relate to each other.

At the beginning of Act Two Rodolfo's conversation is soft, comforting and all embracing except when he is at odds with Eddie. He is obviously a generous romantic. His **dialogue** portrays an open, honest person. His warmth and protectiveness are seen when he attempts to liberate Catherine from Eddie:

'Catherine. If I take in my hands a little bird. And she grows and wishes to fly. But I will not let her out of my hands because I love her so much, is that right for me to do? I don't say you must hate him; but anyway you must go, mustn't you? Catherine?' (p. 46).

The use of 'Catherine' at the beginning and at the end is significant. The first mention of her name draws her in. It shows intimacy. The final 'Catherine' is a request asking for her agreement for an acceptance of their relationship and an end to the claustrophobic entanglement with Eddie.

DIALOGUE OF CONFRONTATION

In the end it is Eddie's uneducated working-class conversation that sounds the most realistic of all the characters. His words are anchored in reality and we realise that he speaks the truth as he sees it. His vision of the truth is twisted but is, nevertheless, true for him. His dialogue is never far away from confrontation and builds relentlessly to the inevitable tragedy at the end of the play.

It is worth looking at the way tension is built and maintained in the dialogue during the final moments of the play. Confrontation is built on confrontation. Beatrice's conversation is soothing, attempting to calm things down but Eddie does not listen. His conversation is shot through with comments that do not allow compromise: 'Didn't you hear what I told you? You walk out that door to that wedding you ain't comin' back here, Beatrice' (p. 60).

Later Marco is in the same uncompromising mood: 'Animal! You go on your knees to me!' (p. 63). Eddie insists that he must have his good name restored: 'You lied about me, Marco. Now say it. Come on now, say it!' (p. 64).

The dialogue carries with it the inevitability of tragedy that may shock, but does not surprise the audience.

EXAMINER'S TIP: WRITING ABOUT MARCO'S LANGUAGE

Marco's conversation tells the audience that he is a serious man who is earnest about his responsibilities. His language informs us of his thoughtful nature. He is also darkly passionate and can be brutally direct when he feels an injustice has been done. At the end of the play he speaks to Eddie a mere five times but each comment is full of venom and intensity.

EXAMINER'S TIP: WRITING ABOUT THE USE OF IMAGERY

Imagery means the creation of pictures in the mind by using figurative language.

We can find two examples in Alfieri's opening speech: 1) 'This is the gullet of New York swallowing the tonnage of the world', and 2) ' ... the flat air in my office suddenly washes in with the green scent of the sea' (p. 4). What other examples can you find?

EXAMINER'S TIP

Keep your own notebook of quotations. This way you will get to know them so well that you will find them far more easily when in the examination.

DID YOU KNOW

The play *The Caucasian Chalk Circle* by Bertolt Brecht should be read by students if only for an examination of the role of 'the singer' who, like Alfieri, is a narrator and commentator – one of whose functions is to offer ideas to the audience to set them thinking.

Structure

A View from the Bridge is a well-structured play with an uncomplicated shape. The play is in two Acts but within these Acts there are a number of easily defined divisions which are controlled by the lawyer, Alfieri. Alfieri is essential to the structure of the play. He opens and closes the play and at other times we see him as Arthur Miller's mouthpiece moving the action quickly onwards.

All the action revolves around Eddie Carbone. His character controls the drama. When he is calm and friendly, the atmosphere reflects this. When he is tense and hostile the atmosphere is uncomfortable. There are a number of flashpoints in the two Acts which echo one another. The controlled hostility at the end of Act One (when Eddie shows Rodolfo how to box and Marco indirectly challenges Eddie) is developed into unpleasant hostility at the beginning of Act Two when Eddie kisses Catherine and Rodolfo. The final explosive violence at the end of the drama is justified when we consider what has gone before.

EXAMINER'S TIP: WRITING ABOUT STRUCTURE AND THEME

Remember that the themes of the play – relationships, justice and the law, manliness (see **Themes**) – are woven into the action and are always part of the fabric of the drama. Arthur Miller moves the action and the themes simply and forcefully throughout the play until he reaches the final tragic scene.

Progress and revision check

REVISION ACTIVITY

① In what way does Eddie's dialogue differ from that of Alfieri?
(Write your answers below)

....

② How would you describe the communication between Eddie and Beatrice?

....

③ How can we tell from Marco's dialogue that he is a thoughtful man?

....

④ Analyse Rodolfo's conversation when he is speaking to Catherine at the
beginning of Act Two. How does it show his warm, protective nature?

....

⑤ In what way can we say that Eddie's speech is uncompromising?

....

REVISION ACTIVITY

On a piece of paper, write down answers to these questions:

● What examples of imagery can you find at the beginning of Act Two?

Start: *An example of imagery is …*

● Describe an example of irony in Eddie's dialogue in Act One.

Start: *An example of irony from Act One is …*

GRADE BOOSTER

Answer this longer, practice question:

Q: In what ways can we say that Alfieri is essential to the structure of the play?
Think about …

● His comments about justice at the beginning.

● Alfieri as a character in the play.

● The way he rounds off the play in his final speech.

For a C grade: You will need to demonstrate that you understand the overall
structure of the play and Alfieri's part in that structure.

For an A grade: You will need to demonstrate that you clearly have insight
into the writer's message and that you can explore the way he uses Alfieri to
construct the play.

PART SIX: GRADE BOOSTER

Understanding the question

Questions in examinations or controlled conditions often need **'decoding'**. Decoding the question helps to ensure that your answer will be relevant and refers to what you have been asked.

 **UNDERSTAND EXAM LANGUAGE**

Get used to exam and essay style language by looking at specimen questions and the words they use. For example:

Exam speak!	Means?	Example
'convey ideas'	*'get across a point to the reader'*: usually you have to say *'how'* this is done.	Miller conveys the idea that justice is a key element behind human behaviour.
'methods, techniques, ways'	The *'things'* the writer does: for example, a powerful description, introducing a shocking event, how someone speaks, etc.	Miller uses many of the techniques of classical tragedy, for example building towards the powerful climax when Marco and Eddie clash near the end of the drama.
'present, represent'	1) present: *'the way things are told to us'* 2) represent: *'what those things might mean underneath'*.	Alfieri is *presented* as a wise figure who *represents* a form of Chorus, commenting on the play's action.

 **'BREAK DOWN' THE QUESTION**

Pick out the **key words** or phrases. For example:

Question: Explore the way Arthur Miller writes about justice in the play. Write about the characters' search for justice, and their feeling that the law is sometimes inadequate.

The focus is on:

- characters and their search for justice as they see it.
- the terrible consequences of their uncompromising attitudes.

What does this tell you?

- **Focus** on Alfieri's comments at the beginning and the end; Eddie's attempts to find a just solution to his problems; his unwillingness to listen to anyone else; Marco's search for revenge; Alfieri's unsuccessful attempts to get both men to listen to reason.

 **KNOW YOUR LITERARY LANGUAGE!**

When studying texts you will come across words such as 'theme', 'symbol', 'imagery' and 'metaphor'. Some of these words could come up in the question you are asked. Make sure you know what they mean before you use them!

Planning your answer

It is vital that you **plan** your response to longer exam questions carefully, and that you then follow your plan, if you are to gain the higher grades.

 ## DO THE RESEARCH!

When revising for the exam, collect **evidence** (for example, quotations) that will support what you have to say. For example, if preparing to answer a question on *A View from the Bridge*, you might list ideas as follows:

Key point	Evidence/quotation	Act/scene/line, etc.
Alfieri sees that compromise and unselfishness is what makes society work.	Alfieri points out that it is better to 'settle for half' because chaos can result if we don't – in this case, Eddie's search for total justice results in his death.	pp. 63 and 64

 ## PLAN FOR PARAGRAPHS

Use paragraphs to plan your answer. For example:

1 The first paragraph should **introduce** the **argument** you wish to make.

2 Then, **develop** this argument with further paragraphs. Include **details**, **examples** and other possible **points of view**. Each paragraph is likely to deal with one point at a time.

3 **Sum up** your argument in the last paragraph.

For example, for the following task:

Question: How does Miller present the character of Rodolfo?

Simple plan:

- Paragraph 1: *Introduction*

- Paragraph 2: *First point*, e.g. Rodolfo's lively, engaging character when he enters.

- Paragraph 3: *Second point*, e.g. Catherine's responses to him.

- Paragraph 4: *Third point*, e.g. The gentle way he treats Catherine at the beginning of Act Two.

- Paragraph 5: *Fourth point,* e.g. His responsible attitude at the end (pages 61–3) when he attempts to prevent the tragedy.

- Paragraph 6: *Conclusion*, e.g. Sum up the points made in the last paragraph, and how this is reflective of Rodolfo's character throughout.

How to use quotations

One of the secrets of success in writing essays is to use quotations **effectively**. There are five basic principles:

❶ Put quotation marks, i.e. ' ', around the quotation.

❷ Write the quotation exactly as it appears in the original.

❸ Do not use a quotation that repeats what you have just written.

❹ Use the quotation so that it fits into your sentence.

❺ Only quote what is most useful.

 **USE QUOTATIONS TO DEVELOP YOUR ARGUMENT**

Quotations should be used to develop the line of thought in your essays. Your comment should not duplicate what is in your quotation. For example:

GRADE D	GRADE C
(simply repeats the idea)	(makes a point and supports it with a relevant quotation)
Eddie asks Rodolfo if he wants to be arrested: 'Look kid; you don't want to be picked up, do ya?'	Miller shows how dangerous it can be if someone sings in the tenement when Eddie says, 'Look kid; you don't want to be picked up, do ya?'

However, the most sophisticated way of using the writer's words is to embed them into your sentence, and further develop the point:

GRADE A

(makes point, embeds quote and develops idea)
Miller shows Eddie's sense of danger and also his hostility when he says to Rodolfo, 'Look, kid; you don't want to be picked up, do ya?' This is a signal to the audience that Eddie dislikes Rodolfo and is also aware that the family might be threatened.

When you use quotations in this way, you are demonstrating the ability to use text as evidence to support your ideas – not simply including words from the original to prove you have read it.

EXAMINER'S TIP

Sometimes it is good to start your answer with a quotation if you feel confident. As an example you might begin with: Beatrice says: 'I don't understand you; she's seventeen years old, you gonna keep her in the house all her life' (p. 11). This could be the beginning of a response to a question about Eddie's relationship with Catherine.

Sitting the examination

Examination papers are carefully designed to give you the opportunity to do your best. Follow these handy hints for exam success:

 **BEFORE YOU START**

- Make sure that you **know the texts** you are writing about so that you are properly prepared and equipped.
- You need to be **comfortable** and **free from distractions**. Inform the invigilator if anything is off-putting, e.g. a shaky desk.
- **Read** the instructions, or rubric, on the front of the examination paper. You should know by now what you need to do but **check** to reassure yourself.
- Before beginning your answer, have a **skim** through the **whole paper** to make sure you don't miss anything **important**.
- Observe the **time allocation** – and follow it carefully. If they recommend 45 minutes for a particular question on a text make sure this is how long you spend.

 **WRITING YOUR RESPONSES**

A typical 40 minute examination essay is probably between 500 and 750 words long.

Ideally, spend 3-4 minutes planning your answer before you begin.

Use the questions to structure your response. Here is an example:

> **Question:** Beatrice is a voice of reason in the play. She is a calming influence but she can also be assertive. Discuss this analysis of the character.

- The introduction could be an overview of the way Beatrice approaches difficult moments created by Eddie;
- the second part could explore the way Beatrice tries to persuade Eddie to behave in a reasonable manner;
- the third part could examine how assertive she can be when necessary;
- the conclusion should sum up your own viewpoint.

For each part allocate paragraphs to cover the points you wish to make (see **Planning your answer**).

Keep your writing clear and easy to read, using paragraphs and link words to show the structure of your answers.

Spend a couple of minutes afterwards quickly checking for obvious errors.

EXAMINER'S TIP

Keep on mentioning the **key words** from the question in your answer. This will keep you on track and remind the examiner that you are answering the question set.

EXAMINER'S TIP

Senior examiners have carried out a survey on the way planning can help to improve grades. They found that planning improved grades significantly in all examinations.

GRADE BOOSTER

When doing your planning for the exam make sure that your notes are clear and not too detailed. If you have too many notes they will merely confuse you.

Responding to a passage from the text

It may be the case that you are asked to answer a question or questions on a short passage from *A View from the Bridge* in the exam. Follow these useful tips for success.

 ## WHAT YOU ARE REQUIRED TO DO

Make sure you are clear when you open the exam paper about:

- The **specific passage you have been given** and the **question(s)** related to it (check that the question you answer is the one about the passage!)

- How **long** you have to write your answer (i.e. 20 minutes?)

- The **sort of question** you have been asked; it is likely to be one in which you have to **show how the writer gets something across to the reader** (for example, the techniques and language Arthur Miller uses to reveal character, setting, theme, etc.).

 ## HOW YOU CAN PREPARE

It might seem that it is difficult to prepare for an 'unseen' passage but you can:

- Select any passage from *A View from the Bridge* of about 300 words. Practise skim reading it quickly and then making notes on:

  ❶ what we learn from the passage

  ❷ the effect of the language used by the writer.

- Practise writing a 20-minute answer based on one of the **Further Questions** at the back of these **York Notes**.

- Use these **York Notes** to check key passages or chapters, reread what makes them important and how the writer creates specific effects.

 ## DURING THE EXAM

Remember:

- **Stick** to the passage and question you have been given. You only have 20 minutes so don't be diverted into other areas.

- Don't panic about **having time** to **read** an 'unseen' passage. The chances are you will **know** the passage or have **already read it** in class or at home.

- The allocated **time** is for reading and **writing**, so make the most of it. You won't have time to plan so quickly read the text and get started!

- The question will expect you to make **close reference** to the given text. This means you should quote **well-chosen words and phrases** from the passage in your answer.

- Keep your quotations **short** and **relevant** to the question.

Improve your grade

It is useful to know the type of responses examiners are looking for when they award different grades. The following broad guidance should help you to improve your grade when responding to the questions you are set!

GRADE C

What you need to show	What this means
Personal, sustained response to task and text	You write enough! You don't run out of ideas after two paragraphs.
Effective use of textual **details** to **support your explanations**	You generally support what you say with evidence, e.g. when Marco raises the chair above Eddie's head Miller tells us that *'Eddie's grin vanishes'* (p. 42) which indicates that Eddie feels threatened.
Explanation of the writer's **use of language, structure, form**, etc., and the **effect on readers**	You must write about the writer's use of these things. It's not enough simply to give a viewpoint. So, you might comment on how **contrasts** are used. For example, Alfieri's speech is thoughtful, educated and controlled while Eddie's dialogue is colloquial and often aggressive.
Convey ideas clearly and **appropriately**	What you say is relevant and is easy for the examiner to follow. If the task asks you to comment on how Catherine is presented, that is who you write about.

GRADE A

What you need to show *in addition* to the above	What this means
Ability to **speculate** about the text and **explore alternative** responses	You look beyond the obvious. You might come up with several explanations for why the play is set in Red Hook, a working class area of New York.
Close analysis and apt selection of **textual detail**	If you are looking at Arthur Miller's use of language, you carefully select and comment on each word in a line or phrase, drawing out its distinctive effect on the reader, e.g. when Eddie says, 'Listen, you been givin' me the willies the way you walk down the street, I mean it' (p. 6). How does each word and emphasis betray Eddie's controlling nature?
Confident and **imaginative interpretation**	Your viewpoint is likely to convince the examiner. You show you have *engaged* with the text, and come up with your own ideas. These may be based on what you have discussed in class or read about, but you have made your own decisions.

Annotated sample answers

This section provides you with extracts from **two model answers**, one at **C grade** and one at **A grade**, to give you an idea of what is required to **achieve** different levels.

Question: What compels Eddie to abandon his beliefs and values?

CANDIDATE 1

Gives a general idea of his reasons

Quotations not embedded

More development required

Shows understanding but does not give real reason for Eddie's comment

Two appropriate quotations to support comments

Near the beginning of the play Eddie asks Beatrice to tell Catherine the story of Vinny Bolzano. He does so in order to impress on Catherine his belief that nobody should 'snitch' on their friends and neighbours to the authorities.

When he does betray the cousins to the Immigration Authorities he does so because he desperately needs to destroy the relationship between Rodolfo and Catherine. When Eddie speaks to Beatrice at the beginning of the play he is quite happy to welcome the immigrants to his home.

He is also making sure that nobody reveals their whereabouts.

'Just remember, kid, you can quicker get back a million dollars that was stole than a word you gave away.' Eddie is talking about people who betray their friends or relatives.

When Eddie hears Rodolfo singing he warns him to be quiet because he might be picked up if someone heard him.

Eddie shows his irritation with Rodolfo and his personality throughout most of the rest of the play. He is not happy when he sees that Catherine likes him. We can see from Alfieri's comments that Eddie's jealousy is interfering with his clear thinking and that there might be trouble looming.

When Marco threatens Eddie and then Eddie sees Catherine and Rodolfo coming out of the bedroom, we know that Eddie is fast losing control. Even so, it is quite a shock to hear him telephoning the Immigration Authorities about Rodolfo and Marco, because of what he said earlier about betrayal. We now see that Eddie has decided that his own interests are more important than those of anyone else.

Arthur Miller builds tension very carefully, mainly through the way he develops Eddie's character from someone who is co-operative and pleasant, to a man who loses control. At the beginning he says to Catherine, 'Well ... I hope you have good luck. I wish you the best. You know that, kid.' Towards the end he says, 'Didn't you hear what I told you? You walk out that door to that wedding you ain't coming back here, Beatrice.'

Eddie's obsession with Catherine and as a result with Rodolfo's and Catherine's relationship drives him over the edge. From the moment he sees Catherine's attraction to Beatrice's cousin he can no longer think logically. It is this that pushes him to forget his loyalty to Beatrice and the two men and, finally, to betray the immigrants to the authorities.

Good use of embedded quotation

Opening sentence of this paragraph focuses on Eddie's attitude

Some appreciation of ideas

Some insight shown here into Eddie's motives

Conclusion rounds off the response quite satisfactorily

Overall comment: This is a sound response which focuses on the question throughout. Some quotations are used appropriately, but more evidence might have improved the grade. The answer shows that the student has some familiarity with the playwright's technique.

GRADE C

CANDIDATE 2

Eddie tells Catherine and Beatrice at the outset that he believes loyalty is very important and anybody who breaks the unwritten code deserves punishment. When he does betray the cousins he makes it quite clear that he feels he, himself, has been betrayed. Beatrice voices what Eddie does not want to hear, his unhealthy relationship with Catherine. It is this relationship, his jealousy of Rodolfo and his own tortured mind which, in the end, force him to abandon his loyalty to the cousins, himself and to his family.

Overall this introduction draws together the important points required for this answer

In his first speech Alfieri sets the tone for the whole play when he says, 'Oh, there were many here who were justly shot by unjust men. Justice is very important here.' He makes the point that justice is much more important than the law. So at the beginning Eddie is saying just that to Beatrice and Catherine. He tells them that even though Rodolfo and Marco are breaking the law they must be protected. He implies that even though they are behaving illegally it would be a betrayal not to protect them. Eddie is making it clear that they must all be on the side of justice.

Well-chosen quote to support an incisive comment

Shows insight into playwright's intention

However, when Rodolfo arrives, Miller shows us Eddie's mood changing quite dramatically and almost immediately. Miller has already made us aware of Eddie's controlling nature when his comfortable relationship with Catherine is threatened even slightly, but now that threat has moved up dramatically when Eddie can see that Catherine is attracted to the Italian. When she tells him that Rodolfo loves her he pleads desperately, 'Don't say that, for God's sake!' And then he tries to cover his grief by saying, 'This is the oldest racket in the country –'

Miller is gradually increasing the tension and whenever Eddie is present on stage we feel that the rumblings under the surface could erupt at any time. From this moment to the end of the play Eddie's mood grows bleaker every time we meet him.

Original evaluation of dramatic devices

Miller uses two moments of high drama which help to heighten Eddie's emotional level even more. When Marco raises the chair above Eddie's head he is warning him and also showing who is the stronger. And, as Miller tells us, 'Eddie's grin vanishes as he absorbs his look'. The second is, of course, when he observes first Catherine and then Rodolfo emerging from the bedroom. Both are terrible moments for Eddie but the second destroys him because he now knows he has lost Catherine for ever. Shocked though we are when he calls the Immigration Authorities, Miller has prepared us for this and we know there is a kind of logic to what Eddie has done.

Sophisticated interpretation

We might feel some disgust at Eddie for the way he has behaved, but, in the end it is difficult to blame him. He has been driven by an obsession that he finds impossible to control. He dare not admit his feelings for Catherine so he has to find other ways of discrediting Rodolfo. It seems obvious in the final moments that he cannot see any way of living and accepting his fate. He has lost Catherine. Beatrice may still love him but part of her despises him, and the whole neighbourhood, as Alfieri says, condemns his actions. You could argue, therefore, that Eddie engineers his own death at the hands of Marco in order to regain some dignity before finally allowing himself to be destroyed and, therefore, ending the terrible torture that he has created for himself.

Shows empathy

Overall Comment: This is a critical and sensitive response. Ideas are conveyed with vigour and are expressed very persuasively. There is evidence of original thinking and this is supported with appropriate evidence in the form of embedded quotations. The playwright's methods are discussed with a light touch. There is a satisfying roundness to the whole answer.

GRADE A

Further questions

EXAM-STYLE QUESTIONS

❶ Compare and contrast the characters of Eddie and Marco.

❷ Examine Miller's ideas about manliness, hostility and aggression as they are portrayed in the play. How are these ideas connected?

❸ Discuss Miller's presentation of the relationship between Eddie and Beatrice. Do you feel that Eddie's feelings for Catherine interfere with this relationship in any way?

❹ What is Alfieri's function in the play?

❺ Compare the characters of Marco and Rodolfo.

❻ Why does Alfieri say that people should 'settle for half'? Is he right to say this?

❼ Write about how Miller presents the relationship between Catherine and Rodolfo. Why does Catherine find Rodolfo attractive?

❽ Discuss the theme of betrayal in *A View from the Bridge*.

❾ How far is Catherine responsible for Eddie's destruction?

❿ Alfieri says Eddie's death is 'useless'. Write your comments on this opinion.

EXTRACT-BASED QUESTIONS

Read the extracts below and then answer the following questions:

❶ (p. 22) 'Eddie: Will you listen a minute' to (p. 33) 'Eddie: I mean if you close the paper fast – you could blow him over'.

- Look closely at what Eddie says here. What does it tell you about his character?

❷ (pp. 41–2) from 'Rodolfo: Dance, Catherine' to the end of the Act.

- With close reference to the extract show how Arthur Miller creates mood and atmosphere.

❸ (p. 49) from 'Alfieri: This is my last word, Eddie' to the bottom of the page.

- With close reference to the extract show how Arthur Miller suggests Alfieri's feelings here.

❹ (p. 54) from 'Eddie: She's got other boarders up there?' to 'They got a temper that family'.

- With close reference to the extract show how Arthur Miller presents Eddie here.

❺ (p. 59) from 'Rodolfo : Marco, tell the man' to (p. 60) 'Alfieri: Only God, Marco'.

- Look closely at what Marco says here. What does it tell you about his character?

Literary terms

Literary term	Explanation
antagonist	the chief opponent of the hero or protagonist in a story; especially used of drama. Thus Marco is the antagonist in *A View from the Bridge*
atmosphere	a common term for the mood – moral, sensational, emotional and intellectual – which dominates a piece of writing
autobiography	the story of a person's life written by that person. Arthur Miller's autobiography is called *Time Bends* and provides valuable background material for the study of *A View from the Bridge*
character	characters are the invented, imaginary persons in a dramatic work which are given human qualities and behaviour
Chorus	in the tragedies of the ancient Greek playwright Aeschylus, the Chorus is a group of characters who represent ordinary people in their attitudes to the action, which they witness as bystanders and on which they comment. Alfieri describes the situation of the play as it occurs and often reacts to the action. Like the Chorus of the Greek theatre he is powerless to affect events
climax	any point of great intensity in a literary work; in a narrative the culminating moment of the action. In *A View from the Bridge* the climax is discovered when Marco turns the knife on Eddie and kills him
colloquialism	the use of the kinds of expression and grammar associated with ordinary, everyday speech rather than formal language. The speech of Catherine, Eddie and Beatrice is regarded as colloquial
dialogue	the speech and conversation between characters in any kind of literary work
empathy	the power to be able to understand how a writer or a character in a play is feeling
figurative	represents an object or an idea by using a metaphor or another figure of speech
flashback	a scene in a play where the narrative suddenly returns to something that has happened in the past
genre	the term for a kind of literature. The three major genres of literature are poetry, drama and the novel (prose); these kinds may be subdivided into many other genres such as narrative verse, tragedy, comedy, short story, etc
gothic	a state of writing that creates a dark, gloomy and depressing atmosphere
imagery	words used to create a picture in the mind
irony	a way of writing in which what is meant is opposite to what the words seem to express. Dramatic irony occurs when the audience is aware of circumstances that are hidden from the characters in the play
melodrama	the most common critical use of the word 'melodrama' or 'melodramatic' is to characterise any kind of writing which relies on sensational happenings, violent action and improbable events. Some critics see *A View from the Bridge* as melodramatic because of its violent ending

Literary term	Explanation
narrator	a storyteller. In a play a storyteller moves the story on quickly by filling in the gaps
pathos	moments in works of art which evoke strong feelings of pity and sorrow are said to have this quality
protagonist	in Greek drama the principal character and actor. Now used almost synonymously with 'hero' to refer to the leading character in a play. Eddie is the protagonist in *A View from the Bridge* though we might argue about the term 'hero' when referring to him
rhetorical (question)	a question that does not require an answer or the answer is contained in the question itself
structure	the overall principle of organisation in a work of literature
style	the characteristic manner in which a writer expresses him/herself, or the particular manner of an individual literary work
theme	an idea that is developed throughout the play
tragedy	possibly the most easily recognised genre in literature and certainly one of the most discussed. Basically a tragedy traces the career and downfall of an individual and shows in this downfall both the capacities and the limitations of human life. The protagonist may be superhuman, a monarch or, in the modern age, an ordinary person. *A View from the Bridge* is regarded as a tragedy by some critics but some have also regarded it as a melodrama
verse play	a play that is written in the poetic form usually in blank verse (i.e. it does not rhyme but it has rhythm) as in the original version of *A View from the Bridge*

Checkpoint answers

CHECKPOINT 1

Justice is the quality of treating people fairly and reasonably.

CHECKPOINT 2

Eddie behaves as he believes a father should behave towards a daughter but his possessiveness does not seem natural.

CHECKPOINT 3

Superficially it seems that Eddie is worried that Rodolfo will be discovered by the Immigration Authorities. In reality, however, he is jealous of Catherine's interest in the Italian.

CHECKPOINT 4

Eddie is afraid Catherine is trying to attract Rodolfo.

CHECKPOINT 5

Rodolfo might be discovered if he goes out too much.

CHECKPOINT 6

Eddie is attempting to discredit Rodolfo.

CHECKPOINT 7

Catherine is afraid that Eddie's suggestion may be true, that Rodolfo may be using his relationship with her for his own ends.

CHECKPOINT 8

Eddie believes a man should not take a girl out without permission.

CHECKPOINT 9

Alfieri speaks directly to the audience about events in the play and he is also a character in his own right. He also acts as a kind of Greek Chorus.

CHECKPOINT 10

Rodolfo reassures Catherine by being totally honest with her about his intentions and about his reasons for becoming an American citizen.

CHECKPOINT 11

Rodolfo is focused, comforting to Catherine and aware of the dangers to the girl if she continues to stay in Eddie's shadow.

CHECKPOINT 12

Beatrice attempts to produce calm in very difficult circumstances.

CHECKPOINT 13

Alfieri means that the law cannot help Eddie.

CHECKPOINT 14

Eddie has earlier criticised Vinny Bolzano, who betrayed his family.

CHECKPOINT 15

Eddie panics because he knows that the Liparis will realise that he is the informer.

CHECKPOINT 16

Marco says: 'That one! He killed my children! That one stole food from my children! (p. 58). Why do you think he says this?

CHECKPOINT 17

Alfieri is waiting for Marco to say he will not take revenge on Eddie.

CHECKPOINT 18

Catherine tries to calm the situation so that Marco will not be sent to prison.

CHECKPOINT 19

Marco believes that he should be allowed to take revenge even if that means breaking the law.

CHECKPOINT 20

Eddie wants his respect back from Marco and the community.

CHECKPOINT 21

Beatrice is still loyal to Eddie.

CHECKPOINT 22

Eddie did not conceal his emotions.